In Between Talking About The Football

By The Same Author

The Shoe

In Between Talking About The Football

Gordon Legge

Polygon
EDINBURGH

© Gordon Legge 1991

First published by Polygon
22 George Square
Edinburgh

Reprinted 1997 (twice)

Set in Linotron Sabon by Polyprint, Edinburgh
and printed and bound in Great Britain by
Redwood Books, Trowbridge, Wiltshire

British Library Cataloguing in Publication Data
Legge, Gordon
In between talking about the football
I.   Title
823'.914 [F]

ISBN 0 7486 61123

The Publisher acknowledges subsidy from the Scottish
Arts Council towards the publication of this volume.

Contents

For Diane and Russell

Summers on the Dole

There was pool, the pool and five-a-side. There were TV, videos and computer games. There were the road trips and the old friends' visits.

The Big Man recalled the stories and The Tank made them funny. Hamish claimed to have done it all and Stuart looked like he had. Wendy never shut up and Grant hardly said a word: Wee Harry's the smartest guy you'd ever meet and Mikey's brains were in his dick.

There were nutters to be avoided, hangers-on to be ignored and casualties to be dumped. Edwyn and English Edgar vetted all newcomers. (Blackballing those who said they could talk about anything. Boring bastards.)

We read lots but only Bukowski was worthy of worship. (As in 'Got drunk. Went to bed. Had a chug. Went to sleep.')

More commonly smashed out skulls, stoned out crates, tripping out boxes, speeding out nuts and, yes, occasionally, shagged out brains.

From black shoes to cool boots to smart trainers. From hating jeans to worn jeans to ripped jeans. From collar-buttoned shirts to workies shirts to baggy, baggy t-shirts. Levi jacket or leather jacket. Everything else just looks stupid.

Brothers and sisters and wonderful parents. And millions and millions of records.

Summer because of the suggestion and cause of the sound of her clothes and the smell of her hair.

Some escaped to London. ('You should get yourself down here.') Some escaped to marriage. ('We never see anybody these days.') A baby was born. ('That's a wild one that. It's better than watching the telly this.') And even The Tank got a job. ('It's all right. It's money, I suppose.')

Probably as shallow as shite but what was the group they

named after us? The Happy Mondays, of course. (E'd out their
faces to a general consensus of 'They're just like us.')

   It's worth thinking about.

   That's long enough.

   And then . . .

I Don't Have Any Friends But I've Got a Cat Called Napalm Death

There he is again. It's raining, I better stop. He's not even got his hood up. *Toot! Toot!* Oh, come on, Tony. Stop pretending you don't see me. Coo-ee. Yes – it is me. Yes – I am offering you a lift. Does the gentleman require written confirmation? Twenty-four hours notice? Passed by the House of Lords? Tony, get a move on, will you. *Do you think I would leave you dyyyy-ingggg* . . . You're not going to get run down. At last. *Watch out!* Jesus! Finally.

'Come on. Get in.'

'Thanks.'

'You're soaked, Tony.'

'It's okay. I'm spongy, I'll absorb it.'

Eh?

'What's up with the bus the day?'

'Well, I missed the 42 so I just got a 26 to the complex and walked. Didn't think it was going to rain, like.'

'That's a two-mile walk, Tony.'

'Done it often enough. Just half an hour into the wind. Save 30p as well. That's three quid a week if I do it all the time. Now that's something that appeals to my nature, cause I'm dead mean, so I am.'

And you're dead weird, Tony. Well weird. That skinny face. A cagoule that's too wee for you. *A brown cagoule.* Those trousers. I don't know. You don't have any shoulders, Tony.

'Is that a new jacket?'

What!?!?

'Eh, yes. Yes, it is. I got it on Saturday.'

'Pretty smart. It looks new.'

What does that mean? Everything I wear is new.

'I'm hopelesss with clothes. My mum still buys mine.'

Hey, Jesus. Look, I hope you're not one of those freaks that memorizes everything. Tell me you're not a freak, Tony. I mean it. Please, tell me you're not a freak.

'God, I hate cars. They smell like perfumed armpits.'

!?!

'That rain's fair coming down now. I'm quite glad I got this lift off you, actually. This thing isn't waterproof.'

'You might have caught pneumonia, Tony.'

'Nah, I've never had a cold for eight years.'

That's true. You only catch colds from people. How old are you, Tony?

'How old are you, Tony?'

'Eh, thirty.'

Thirty! Thirty? *Thirty.*

'Look, Tony, if you'd have waited five minutes there would've been another bus right out. I don't grudge you the lift or anything, I'm just curious as to why you didn't hang on.'

'I'm not one for hanging about. I like the exercise. You don't get much with this job. You just sit on your arse all day doing nothing. And I really am mean. I never use the canteen either. Place just stinks of dead animals, anyway. Nah, I'd rather walk and I'd rather eat my pieces.'

'I suppose so. But you miss out on all the exciting social life of the canteen.'

'I get enough of that during working hours, thank you very much. See if I hear one more woman going on about her hysterectomy . . . Is that all you women ever talk about?'

!!!

'Well . . . Blast! Did you see that? Right in front of me. FUCKING ARSE! Ever heard of priority, matey?'

'You don't lose your temper when you're walking, by the way.'

I knew you'd say that, Tony. Just as you knew I'd smile. You've got a nice smile, Tony. And you've got beautiful eyes. You've got your good points. You're obviously very intelligent.

'Do you have a girlfriend, Tony?'

'Nah. Got a cat, though.'

'Oh. What's it called?'

'Eh . . . Napalm Death.'

'*What?*'

'It's named after a group. I don't think you'd like them.'

'I'll take your word for it. What do you do? What's your hobbies and that?'

'Eh. Read tons. Play with my toys. Watch telly and videos. I miss my pals, really. Don't have any friends in the big city yet.'

'I'm sure you'll fit in.'

'Don't know if I want to. Don't like being grown up. I've been a manic depressive since my mam bought me long trousers.'

What am I supposed to say to that? And men wonder why women always ask questions.

'There's a space. Quick.'

'I see it. I see it. I'm not blind, Tony.'

'Well, if you don't mind me saying so, thank fuck for that.'

Ha ha. Uh-oh. We're getting pretty serious eye contact here. Look, Tony, I don't want to . . . Tony, don't look down the front of my blouse, you'll only see a beige bra . . . I don't want to give you lifts anymore. Some of the girls have been saying things, just jokes and that. I mean you're not grotesque or anything. Oh, it would probably be for the best if I lied. Think of something. I bet you're hung like a truncheon, Tony.

'Did you see that programme on child slavery last night?'

Oh, shut up, will you . . . Hey, that would explain the trousers.

'Eh, no. No, I was out. Was it good?'

'Good isn't the right word. Though I suspect television isn't the right medium either.'

I give up. Work at last. Saved. Right, Tony, you go your way, I go mine.

'Well, thanks for the lift. You're a smashing wee driver. Heh heh. Much appreciated and all that shit . . . Eh, I'm sorry, I don't know your name.'

What? Everybody knows me.

'*Jacqui*, it's Jacqui.'

'Really! Well, eh, thanks, Jacqui. I'll maybe see you later.'

Oh God. He's smiling. He's lingering . . .

Two Days till Sheila, Three Days till Celtic

The clatter of the letter-box was enough to rouse the dead and the envelope hit the floorboards with the gentlest of pats.

Pushing the duvet from his forehead, Craig noted it was quarter-past nine and flicked on the radio. Simon Mayo and Cybil Roscoe were talking about mini-skirts. Craig listened to their cosy pillow-talk until the start of the next record then, in one movement, wrapped the bedcover around himself and leapt out of bed.

After feeding the cat and making himself a cup of tea he went through to the living-room. There, kneeling in front of the electric fire and listening to the Van Morrison tape they'd had on last night, Craig supped his tea and demolished the rest of the shortbread Sheila'd brought round.

Twenty pound had been docked off his giro: the electricity board. Eighteen months' worth of small estimates had been followed by an entrance demand then a request for £280. Craig had all but ignored this so now they got his money at source. The council had mucked him about as well. Craig had amassed a fair bit of arrears while he was working and now they wanted a fiver a week. He was only supposed to pay £3.88 a fortnight since his unemployment benefit had run out and he was now on income support. The introduction of the Poll Tax confused him further. Somebody told him it meant he would be paying less. All Craig wanted was for no one to pay so that he could get lost in the crowd, like the TV licence. But it didn't take away the arrears. That's how they always got you. See them the day, Craig reminded himself. That wee fascist with the South African moustache.

The 'Pope's Eleven' t-shirt, black Puma bottoms, biker's jacket and £50 Reeboks – Craig's clothes – were freezing. They made his arms and legs shiver, as though taking clothes off rather than putting them on. Craig lit a cigarette. Sheila'd left two last night. The tape finished and Craig switched the mode to FM.

Mott the Hoople, 'Roll Away The Stone' . . . *The Golden Year, 1973. Yesss. We won the league but they beat us in the cup. 3-2. Tam fucking dickhead Forsyth. Eighteen inches and the divvy nearly missed. Jammy bastards.*

Whilst washing and shaving Craig thought through the money he owed. The council and Hammy would each get a fiver the day. Sheila was owed a couple of quid but she wouldn't hassle him for it. Then there was the money for his mum's catalogue. Craig didn't want to think any further. That was enough to be going on with.

Craig decided to put on an LP before he left and chose Lowell George's *Thanks, I'll Eat It Here*. During the gap between 'Honest Man' and 'Two Trains' he switched to the radio and then back again.

Eh, 'I'm A Tiger', Lulu . . . oh, fuck, eh . . . '68. I think. Yeah. That's it. That's right. That's right. Eh . . . we won the league and Dunfermline won the cup. Beat us in the first round. At home, Christ.

To the amusement of the cat Craig practised his keepie-uppie with the wee green ball while the rest of the LP played out. Craig was pleased with his progress. He was now confident with both feet and could incorporate his knees, chest and head. Roll on the summer league.

On his way down the town, Craig met Stevie Roy and got a wave from Duncan Reid. It wasn't as cold as Craig had expected. The weather was seldom as bad as it looked from his window. His flat never got the sun. Even so, Craig resolved to put the electric fire back in the cupboard later. Stop Sheila lecturing him about staying in all day and running up bills. He'd play more keepie-uppie when he was cold. Start doing press-ups again as well.

The queue at the post office was as long as ever, and Craig waited impatiently, silently cursing the 'bugsy wee women' in front of him who seemed to take forever. Once Craig had collected his money he went next door and paid the council. The SSEB was next along but the woman who worked there

was a friend of his mother's and Craig didn't want to risk
further mentions in that particular bad book. He just wanted
to pay weekly like everyone else did, or get those powercard
things. To start again. Sheila told him it was all his own
fault, same with the council. She could be a bit niggly at
times.

At the Co-op, Craig bought bread, biscuits, milk, marge,
catfood, beans, soup, a half-pound of cheese and a jar of Red
Mountain coffee. Sheila had teased him about getting that
chicory shit. Craig got a shock when the total appeared on the
till: £6.82. Her and her Red Mountain coffee, Craig mumbled
to himself. A few things out of Farmfoods and that would be
him. Should do a while, Craig thought. It would have to. He
couldn't even go round to his folks to scrounge food on
account of the catalogue situation. Craig reminded himself he
was needing shaving-foam. He'd get that during the week.

*Get that out of Boots. I'll nick some of those vitamin pills
again. Saves me having to bother too much about eating.
Right, meet Hammy in the pub at eleven. Go to the Job Centre
first . . . Still plenty of jobs in Oban. Not much else. Can't even
smoke in here these days. Shit, forgot to get fags! Just get them
in the pub. 11p dearer. Stop! You've got to stop. Sheila's going
to. A week on Tuesday, she says.*

Hammy was sitting at the bar. He was as fat and relaxed as
Craig was skinny and intense.

'How you doing, sir?' asked Craig.

'Fine. Fine. Yourself?'

'Eh, okay. There's that money, by the way. You want a
drink?'

Hammy indicated the near full pint he was nursing and said
he was all right. The barmaid appeared carrying boxes of
crisps and Craig bellowed out 'Pint of Guinness, please,
Wilma. And twenty Regal. And you got change for the
jukebox and the pool?'

'In a minute, Craig,' said Wilma, wearily. There were no
other customers in the pub.

'This you treating me to a game of pool?' said Hammy,
indicating playful surprise by raising his eyebrows.

'Yeah. Why not? That was good of you with that fiver and that. I really needed it.'

'You're all right, I suppose,' said Hammy, although his eyebrows didn't seem so sure. He gave a knowing laugh and added, 'Better than some I could name, anyway.'

'You're telling me. You been next door?'

'Nah, that place is hopeless. I'll tell you what, though, I hear they might be starting up a new contract at Mossmorran. Our lot were at the last one. You interested, like?'

'Yeah, sure. You being serious? I'd be well into that. I mean, I need to get my head thegether.' Craig paused before adding, 'I really mean it this time.'

Hammy left the sarcasm to his eyebrows as he said, 'Well, I'll see my brother about getting you a form.'

'Oh, that would be great.' Craig looked pleased. 'Do you want to rack-up while I check out what's on the jukebox?' Craig handed some change to Hammy.

'You want to play for money?' Hammy stood up and tucked his t-shirt and his arse into his jeans.

'No way, sir. I've never beat you playing for money.'

Craig selected five tracks from *The Story of The Clash Vol. I* off the CD jukebox, a quid. He was thinking about Mossmorran.

Fitter's mate, welder's mate. Stand about doing nothing. Clear two hundred a week, easily. Get the big dosh to get myself sorted out. See off the bills and debts. Best to get in with Hammy and this lot. He knows the score.

They played three games of pool. Craig won two and Hammy bought him a pint. Steve Johnson off the Celtic bus and a couple of his mates came in. They'd heard about the Mossmorran contracts and the big wages. Craig got anxious when they mentioned their previous experience and all their skills. Hammy told him not to worry and just to say he'd worked as a fitter's mate. Hammy would help him out. Craig felt reassured. He'd never worked on the sites before. He'd always looked down on the workies with their dirty clothes. It was a bit bugsy. Now that he knew a few of them, though, it was all right. They were just normal blokes, most of them.

They told stories about being on the rigs and on the continent. Presently, they were wanting to get involved with the Channel Tunnel. Twelve hundred quid a week, they said. Craig didn't need that kind of money. He just wanted to clear his debts. Which reminded him he better be going. Craig said his farewells and told Hammy he'd be in touch about the form.

As Craig headed through the shopping precinct to Farmfoods, he bumped into Kev Lawson.

'Hi, Craigie,' said Kev. 'How you doing? Fancy coming round the night?'

'Eh . . .'

'It's just that I'm lined up for a half-quarter. Do you fancy going halfers?'

'Eh, I dunno, really.'

'Nice bit of black. It's really mellow. Good stuff. I had a wee smoke of some last night at Bob and Senga's.'

'Yeah. I heard there was a good bit doing the rounds . . . I think I'll give it a bye, though. I'm a bit short just now, like.'

'Okay. It's up to you. How you doing, anyway? You should pop round some time.'

'Yeah, I'm fine.'

'Well, pop round then. We'll get stoned and have a game of Subutteo.'

'Will do. Next week, maybe.'

'Name a day then.'

'Eh, Tuesday. Ha, I'll be skint by then.'

'Right. Tuesday. Great. By the way, how's Sheila?'

'Oh, she's getting on fine. She's brilliant.'

'Good. This you with the messages then. Great dinners on giro day, eh? The plate's never big enough.'

'That's right, yeah.'

'Anyway, pop round and see us. Are the rest of the team in the pub?'

'Yeah, a few of them. Eh, Hammy, Steve, Shuzz and Robbie are in.'

'Right, Craigie, well, take care of yourself, man.' Kev put his arm around Craig's shoulder and said, 'Look, sir, you should just fuck the messages and come back to the pub. I'll stand you a pint.'

'Nah, not the day.'

'Okay. Well, I'll see you later then, Craigie.'

'Right, see you.'

A few more pints down the pub, see about scoring a bit of dope then a taxi home. That's what it was usually like. Then that great big meal. Sometimes a fish supper cause you were too drunk to be bothered making a meal. More often than not you were too drunk to do either and you crashed out in front of the fire before eight o'clock. But within the fortnight you were having to get loans to go and see Celtic. Craig got treated to a few pints by the lads that worked. They never grudged it. Craig had treated folk when he was working. That's the way things went.

Back in the pub they would be laughing and joking, shunting back and forwards to the bookies and playing pool. Soon the guys would be in off the early shift – Sean and Bill would be there. Then later the boys of the day shift. Somebody would stick Runrig on the CD jukebox and Craig and Sean would go daft, shouting, 'How can anyone listen to that shit?'

Craig had intended to get pies, chips and a Black Forest gâteau as a surprise for Sheila when she came round on Friday. But as he looked around him at the shops and the 'bugsy wee women' Craig thought about them back in the pub and of his cold flat. He wanted to go back to the pub and he wanted to save his money for Sheila and Celtic. Sheila lectured him all the time about money. It was all right for her; she had a job. It shouldn't be a decision to enjoy yourself with your mates, Craig told himself. Like Tam Forsyth's shitty wee goal, it just wasn't fair.

Craig made up his mind to tell Sheila the good news about Mossmorran on Friday as he headed back to the pub. A few spots of rain threatened to mess his immaculate hair as if to confirm he'd made the right decision.

Neither Through Spite nor Tease

'Right, thanks.' June smiled in the direction of the bus driver as she descended the steps. The smile disappeared, however, as she turned and saw the car parked at the far end of the cul-de-sac. Shit. He was in.

She'd had the cleaning job six weeks, Tuesday and Friday mornings. The pay was good but the bloke – a pensioner, ex-serviceman, RAF – was a tramp and a bit of a crackpot. His own family had contacted June and told her not to take the job. *His own family.*

The houses round here were beautiful: all detached, with conifer trees in the front gardens. There was no litter, save some red chips spreading from driveways and the obligatory milk-bottles nestling in the bushed area at the entrance. Typically, the only thing that could be vandalised had been vandalised: the street sign at the corner was bent and twisted, and etched with lovers' initials and gang loyalties.

Even the house at the far end was impressive. The garden, though, bore no trees, flowers or shrubs. It was just a lawn. A stark, intimidating lawn. Roughly the size of an eighteen-yard box, it was perfectly level and beautifully green. It looked like Wembley on Cup Final day, as though it had been vacuumed. His pride and joy.

Hope he's going out, June said to herself. Don't want to talk to him. Don't even want to see him. The bloke scared June. He was grumpy and made a show of being uninterested in June and all she had to say. He told her she was 'shallow' and how he, on the other hand, had made 'discoveries' and knew 'something'. This information, he said, had been written down and passed on to his lawyers, who would make public the contents only after his death. This was something that would change the world, he told June. June wasn't fascinated. She wasn't even bothered. She figured he'd been a spoilt bastard all his life and that he was ignorant. She hated people like that. They were always the ones with the money.

June rapped the door and, as usual, just let herself in. The stink was horrendous. *Vomit.* The stairs in front of her were covered in it, shining like spilt paint on the worn carpet. June opened the door fully and then went through to the kitchen. She donned her rubber gloves and grabbed a roll of blue paper before going upstairs.

She discovered him asleep on his bed, snoring loudly and irregularly, as messy and shameless as one of her old patients. The stairs had taken the brunt of it but his hair, face, shirt and bedclothes were matted and stained, indicating he'd been sick again through the night.

June opened the three windows and gulped fresh air then lifted his dentures from the floor of the massive bedroom and put them in a mug of water on the dresser. After rolling him on his side, June removed the bedclothes and his shirt. She took these, and his jumper, downstairs and deposited them in the automatic. Before heading back up she opened the rest of the windows.

In the bathroom there was a splash of what her youngest called arse-sauce on the linoleum. Mercifully, he'd managed to get most of it in the pan. The blue paper came into action and she cleaned it up. For a second June feared that he might have been caught short during the night. No. No, she'd have smelt that.

Using a sponge and soapy water, June quickly gave a wash to his scalp and his face. His face looked exhausted, as well it might.

The stairs were next.

In the kitchen cupboard June found the wire-brush and finally made use of one of the millions of polybags he filled the drawers with. For the next half-hour she was on her hands and knees, scrubbing away and collecting the debris in the polybag, frequently cursing herself as she tore the worn carpet with her efforts. To neutralize the smell as much as anything, June gave a cursory wash to the carpet using some strong disinfectant. To finish with, she used the blue paper to wipe the skirting-boards.

For the rest of the morning June hurriedly carried out her normal duties: tidying the living-room, polishing the spare bedrooms and scrubbing the kitchen. She rewarded herself with a break and relaxed with a cup of coffee, a vanilla slice and two Classic biscuits. She smoked one of his fags as she studied her bus timetable. By this time the wash-cycle was complete and June hung the washing out to dry. When she came in, she remembered to put the roll of blue paper in her bag.

That just left the hoovering. June went upstairs and brought the machine down. She did the downstairs bedroom first. Opening all the doors and windows had made the house cold and given June a headache. Her shoulders were sore and she felt tired and nauseous, longing for a bath and a change of clothes. But Campbell had to be picked up from her mother's at two then she had to see the council about the dampness at four.

June swung the cable over her shoulders and set to hoovering the living-room. There was more furniture in here than there was in the rest of the house put together. Why he had so many tables and chairs was a mystery to June. It was as though he was preparing for a party, or a group of visitors.

June skilfully cleaned out every last corner while managing not to bash the furniture. She noted that the bag needed changing and did this before heading upstairs.

After fitting on the appropriate extension, June started to work her way down the stairs. When she reached half-way the power went off.

June looked up to see him standing at the top of the stairs in his string vest and trousers, silhouetted by the sunlight coming through the window.

'Look,' he said. 'I'm sorry about the mess.' Then he smiled in a smug, unforgiving way and added, 'I used to take a good bucket when I was younger. I don't feel guilty if that's what you're trying to make me do!' Gingerly, he made his way down and motioned June into the living-room.

June sat down and helped herself to another of his fags without him noticing. He remained standing. Abruptly, he turned and pointed a finger at June. 'Well, let me tell you, dear,' he said, 'I had a great time last night.'

June said nothing but her fingers were crossed.

'Why have you done all this?' he added, getting angry. 'I know what a state this place was in. You could have just taken your wages. You know where I leave them.'

June shrugged her shoulders.

'Why?' he repeated.

'Don't know,' said June. 'Maybe you remind me of my dad.'

'Ha. Did he like the bevvy?'

'Nah. He was teetotal.'

'You noising me up?' he said. 'Taking the rise out of me. You're enjoying this, eh?'

June looked out the window and said, 'I'll be needing more blue paper. Your windows are filthy.'

'Yes, surely.' He looked ill again. As if getting angry had broken down his resistance to the pain. 'Look, I'll . . . I'll get you more blue paper, all right? I'll phone my brother-in-law the night and get you more blasted blue paper. Here, take this, and, well, you know where your wages are.'

His family had been right. June took the three twenty-pound notes, the tenner and the two fivers and put them in the envelope with her twenty-pound wage.

A Tin of Pears, A Lump of Cheese
and Stewed Tea

My grandfather was a communist; that's what they said, anyway. He used to babysit me till I was thirteen. My folks got their night out and I got pears, cheese and stewed tea.

After being dropped off at his bit in the early evening, I would immediately set about starting up the big coal fire. This was my job. Once it was alight we would stare into it and talk about it. When it was fully ablaze my grandfather relaxed back into his armchair but I would be up as close as I could, closer than a cat, hoping my face would tan.

He asked me about school and how I was getting on. There was never much to say. I was really ordinary and bored by school. He, though, always went on about how clever I was and how smart I was.

My grandfather seldom watched television and had few visitors, and they were exclusively male and elderly. He told me everything and everything couldn't have been much cause he kept on repeating himself. Mostly it was about politics and history.

'Do you want some cheese?'

'Aye.'

'Well, wash your hands then.'

Then he cut a great big lump of cheese into ten pieces and poured the tea.

'Help yourself.'

'Great.'

The tea was disgusting. What he did was to make a big pot in the morning and heat it up as and when required on the hearth. *It was vile.* Only OD'ing on Parmesan has ever come close. It took me two hours to sip half a mugful.

I always got six bits of cheese to his four while he rabbited on about politics and history. Politics made him mad. He hated politicians, the rich, the English, the Royal Family and the Empire. He hated the lorries and the flats. He hated Glasgow cause it was full of tinks and Edinburgh cause it was full of snobs. He hated a lot. I heard all about colonialism and divide and rule from him. I heard that expression more than any other. He asked me if I'd seen the starving children on television and told me that's what divide and rule did. Whenever I came across the poor, he told me, I should recall what he said about divide and rule, regardless of how stupid, selfish, dirty or awful they were. This was strange because my grandfather was quite scathing about the local tramps and drunks. When he saw one passing outside, he would bolt from his chair and rush over to the window. I got quite frightened by this show of disgust. I don't know why he did it. Maybe they ruined his theories or there was something personal. I don't know. Another favourite expression was finite. He got me to count things, to put a number on them, then he told me you could put a number on all the starving, all the poor and all the problems. Solving the problems was as easy as counting, he said.

The fire would die down and we'd watch the red bits disappear and I'd crumble the white bits with the poker. He never kept the fire stoked up. I had to act cold for him to tell me to start up a new one. While I was doing this he would go through to the kitchen. I'd hear the grinding of the tin-opener followed by *Splash! Splash!*

'Want some pears?'

'Aye.'

'You know what to do then.'

So I would go and wash my hands.

'There you go.'

'Great.'

I'd be back in front of the fire while my grandfather raved on.

He went on about history and said how he wished he'd studied history more, cause that's where the problems came from. You used it to solve practical problems and you called it experience. He said that the working class and the Africans had been denied a history, so they were disadvantaged.

I can recall all this because I heard it so often. I liked looking through atlases and the *Guinness Book of Records*, and he kind of exploited that.

I went through a period of not liking my grandfather and resenting him. I resented him cause I missed out on playing football on Saturday mornings, and he put a lot of pressure on me by going on about how smart I was. When I told him I couldn't study history at school because only the top people got in that class, he was really disappointed. He said I would be studying geography then. No, I told him, I was in the Modern Studies class. I had to explain to him what that was.

He only took me to the football a few times; interminably poking my shoulder and pointing into the crowd and saying 'Now, do you know who that man is? . . . No . . . Well, that's a man called . . .' I told him I couldn't see so I left him and went down the front. After the match we went to a fancy restaurant and had tea and cream cakes. He never bought meals. He never had juice or sweets in the house. At the football I got two boiled sweets, one for each half.

I don't remember doing anything with my grandfather other than listening to him; we never walked or fished or went away on bus trips or did anything like that; he never had any pets; he never gave me any toys, just big history books and atlases. I never read the history books although I told him that I did. He was really proud of his presents. It was easy for me to pretend I'd read them. I just needed to nod and say 'That's right' and leave all the talking to him.

'Time for your bed.'

'Suppose so.'

I would stay the night and get to watch TV on Saturdays. Strange programmes in the morning and the horse-racing and the wrestling in the afternoon. If I picked winners in the horse-racing he would give me 5p. I always backed favourites unless there was a white horse. We supported Andy Robin and Les Kellet in the wrestling. My grandfather would roar with laughter when Les Kellet was on.

By this time, my folks had arrived to pick me up. My mum got really involved with the wrestling while my dad waited impatiently for the football results and always refused the offer of our tea.

My grandfather was my mother's father. Him and my dad didn't hit it off. My dad said he was mean, and that he was a communist.

As I grew older I saw less and less of my grandfather. He wasn't one for going out and when the babysitting was no longer required I only ever seen him at the festive season, still talking about the same old things. When I moved out of the town I lost touch with him altogether. On my Christmas and New Year visiting-list he was well down. I always intended to go and see him but the nights are long and the days are spent recovering over that week.

It's the way of things, though, that home's where you head for when there's trouble. Now I'm back here living in a flat, less than two hundred yards from the one I was brought up in. If you go over the bridge then through the four-in-a-block estate and across the main road, you come to a a sheltered housing scheme. This is where my grandfather now lives.

He's a fair age now and despite a few pains he's quite happy and a lot friendlier than I ever recall him being, unbelievably flirting with the female residents. He talks a lot more about himself these days. Thinking about it, I grew up knowing next to nothing about him, his own life. I never knew he'd been in the Far East during the Second World War and I was shocked to discover that he'd been married twice. He says he was a member of the Communist Party when he was younger but not anymore. He doesn't like the present government or the opposition *at all*. They're all obsessed with money, he says. In his day people made do. They made their own entertainment; now the kids can't go out cause everything costs so much. It's not their fault, he says.

My grandfather still goes on about how smart and clever I am. He tells me there's a connection between us and shows me some writing he did when he was younger. They're just quotes or paragraphs written on various pieces of paper, anything that was handy. He says some of them were copied from newspapers and some from books but most, he thinks, were his own. Things about history, opinions, stories and jokes. I found them difficult to read and they tended to be about people or incidents of which my knowledge could be said to be somewhat vague. The handwriting is tiny, though. I like that.

These days my grandfather gives me books on football. It's football we mostly talk about. I went round there last night after Rangers signed Mo Johnston. We were both very happy. My grandfather said he was going to write to Graeme Souness and congratulate him. He told me to keep an eye open because a lot of changes were going to take place in the world following this minor miracle. He told me he knew his history and that's what happened.

We sat all night anticipating the changes as he refilled our mugs with tea from the big pot and heated them in the microwave. Still vile but I can take it these days.

Holy Willie Bob! Buries It! Goal!

Holy Willie Bob was disappointed. Big Diddy was supposed to be going out with his sister, but at last night's party Big Diddy was seen to be chasing after young Nicki Cook. Time and time again Holy Willie Bob had warned her this would happen; but she'd still fallen head over heels for the six-foot-four philanderer who was acknowledged by even his best friends to be something of a one-off in the fucking moron stakes.

The game got underway and soon proved itself to be *shite*. Andy was still feeling the effects of last night's speed. Hyperactive at the best of times, he bombed everywhere and never passed the ball to anyone. Scottie, on the other hand, had to leave the hall every five minutes to throw up. An inconvenience which appeared to cause him no end of mirth. Sumo took great pride in the fact he smoked forty fags a day, never walked further than his car and ate red meat for dessert. Equally, he regarded himself as something of a serious drinker – as opposed to the effete, loutish 'social drinker' – but today he felt like he was insides-out and somebody was slashing at his intestines with broken glass. He was suffering and he called it alcohol poisoning. Roddy and Murray had nicked somebody's dope and skinned up a few joints for the morning after. Every time the ball came near them they took to the giggling. Sandy was a sad and depressing git at the best of times but today he surpassed himself. He'd missed the party on account of him having to work the night shift and would not stop going on about how pissed-off this had made him. The party had been held in honour of Jimmy who was back from Leeds for the weekend. The last time he'd been this drunk had been his going-away party. He crouched in the goalmouth terrified the ball would come near him. Brian was doing stretching exercises in the other goalkeeping position. He had been the host of the party and had remained sober throughout.

He had half a mind to abandon the game and just head off to the pool. He was fearful, though, that somebody would drown. From the way Sandy was getting on everybody's nerves, the said drowning would not necessarily have been of an accidental nature.

They played like they talked: they interrupted each other, they ignored each other and they slagged each other to high hell. Like their professional counterparts they played with what has come to be known as passion, i.e. they moaned all the time, they were forever in the huff and the physical contact wasn't far off assault.

Sumo wasn't happy about Roddy wearing that '5-1' t-shirt and man-marked him in the literal sense. Andy was in a world of his own and embarked on mazy dribbles that would forever land him boxed in the corner. Whereupon Scottie would come crunching in and smash him against the wall. Just a shoulder charge, Scottie said. Sandy whinged all the time cause nobody passed the ball to him. When he did achieve possession he tried a series of long-range shots that never went anywhere near the target. He then screamed 'BASTARD' and stamped his feet on the ground. Murray never passed the ball to Holy Willie Bob since Murray himself had a wee bit of a hankering for Holy Willie Bob's sister and blamed Holy Willie Bob for her taking up with his arch-rival, Big Diddy. Holy Willie Bob wanted to change the sides to make them fairer, and cause he didn't like being on the same side as Murray who never seemed to pass the ball to him.

Big Diddy just blootered the ball every time he got it. This made Holy Willie Bob mad. Cause for Holy Willie Bob, football was not merely, as Bill Shankly had claimed, more important than life or death, it was in the same league as the hereafter. Whether debating the politics, comparing the players, analysing the results or just playing their weekly wee game of five-a-side, Holy Willie Bob was as serious as he was on Sunday mornings.

Big Diddy lifted the ball and aimed his shot upwards, trying to get the ball stuck in the skylight. Holy Willie Bob had had enough and screamed 'Will you get it thegether?' Startled, the others looked on at his outburst. They thought Holy Willie Bob was fuming cause of the shit between Big Diddy and young Nicki Cook. Holy Willie Bob, however, blocked out everything when he was playing football, and was concerned solely with preventing the game from developing into a shambles. Big Diddy said, 'Calm down. Calm down.' Holy Willie Bob said, 'Come on then.' Holy Willie Bob meant, 'Let's get back to the game' but everybody thought he was squaring up to Big Diddy. Big Diddy said, 'Look, I'm not into this,' as Holy Willie Bob came striding over towards him, ostensibly to retrieve the ball but everybody thought he was preparing to launch an attack on Big Diddy. He stopped. Big Diddy repeated, 'I told you, I'm not into this.' Holy Willie Bob said, 'Well, fuck off then.' (Holy Willie Bob was not averse to swearing when it came to football and meant for Big Diddy to take leave of the game but everybody thought Holy Willie Bob was telling Big Diddy to finish with his sister.) Big Diddy lowered his head and said, 'Listen, I'm sorry about last night. I was really pissed and I'm ashamed of myself. Nothing happened. I'm telling you straight, *nothing happened*. I care about Carol a lot. I really do. Take it easy, wee man. You're all right. I'd even take you for a brother-in-law.' Holy Willie Bob suddenly became aware of what was going on. He'd always known God moved in mysterious ways – everybody knew that – but Holy Willie Bob had long suspected that God kept an eye on every game of football. Well, now it was confirmed. Just as though he'd scored a goal, the initial surprise changed to an arrogant swagger and Holy Willie Bob declared with the faith of the true believer, 'Right then. Is this a game of football or what?'

Upstairs, Downstairs

'I suppose they'll be back from the club later.' As usual I regret opening my mouth.

Karen glares at me and says, 'Oh, thanks for reminding me, *bud*.'

That's her unaffectionate name for me. She gets up and stretches to the ceiling then goes through to the kitchen.

It's the old couple upstairs, you see. They go out on Friday nights and get drunk. Then they come home and enact a major battle right above our heads.

This is our first house. I got it through the work. We got hundreds of wedding presents and wanted for nothing; we're bringing in good money; we maintain a nice garden – and I'm erecting a greenhouse; the neighbours are friendly – we like them cause they like us, basically; we're that 'nice young couple that just moved in'. Everything's cosy and rosy apart from upstairs.

First, we discovered that their creaky floorboards were creaky all the time. Then it was their squeaky bed and their snorty snoring. These things are fairly normal: Friday nights aren't. We soon had to accept that what happens on Friday nights was going to happen every Friday night. There's his shouting and her screaming, then his slamming and her crying. It's scary as well as annoying. They've two grown-up sons, both married and living on the other side of town. One Friday when it was particularly bad I got the number of one of them out of the book and gave him a call. He came round but that only made things worse. He's the man's son from a previous marriage and he and his father had one hell of a barny. I told Karen if anything like that happened again I was going to phone the police. She doesn't believe me. She says that when I'm trying to be assertive I do a good impression of Mr Barraclough out of *Porridge*.

'It's ridiculous, this,' says Karen returning with two mugs of coffee and a packet of Abernethys. 'They're fucking deaf as well. See the volume he has that telly at. God, if I hear that McEwan's Lager advert again, I'll be the one that's screaming.' She snaps an Abernethy like it's somebody's neck.

'Which one's that?' I ask, pretending I don't know.

'The one with the chins.' Karen tries to turn her head upside down.

The first time I spoke to him I happened to mention that we'd honeymooned in Dublin. This got him going and he went on about his great love for Ireland and his fond memories. From what he was saying I gathered that his trips were fairly regular. I asked why. He eyed me with suspicion and declared, 'For the marching, son. For the marching.' As if it could have been anything else. Me and Karen had a good laugh afterwards when I told her.

On Fridays we see them heading off in the evening. At six foot four he's pretty impressive with his straight back and military gait (all that marching). Immaculate in suit and tie, his hair and shoes vye for the title of shiniest accessory. His wife swaps her fawn raincoat for a fur coat when they go out at night. Although only in her fifties, she's very frail; walking as though wearing high heels for the first time, she clings onto her husband's arm, babbling constantly. Sometimes we see them out separately: her going to the shops and him going for a walk. They both stop and talk but she gossips. From what we gather, nobody cares much for him and she's in and out of hospital all the time.

'I'd really like them to drop dead,' announces Karen. 'For the first time in my life I hate an old person so much I wish they'd curl up and croak.' Karen snaps two Abernethys in two. 'Oh, it would be great. They could renovate upstairs and get those floorboards sorted. It would be months before they got anyone new in. Bliss.'

'I'd settle for them moving.'

'They won't move. They won't die either. Well, she will, he won't. She's just as bad as him. Her and her nerves. For somebody that's supposed to be bothered with nerves, she doesn't half scream her head off.'

'It could be a lot worse, Karen, think of the trouble your sister's been having.'

'Of course. Of course. But I'm a selfish bitch and I want them dead.' Karen gives a fiendish laugh and inserts a whole Abernethy into her mouth.

'Do you want to go out?' I ask.

'Nah. We've got *Cheers, Friday Sportscene* and *Scotsport Extra Time* on the night. This is the night all good punks get to stay in and hurl abuse at Chic Hun.' Karen is a punk and a Celtic supporter. A punk by vocation and a Celtic supporter since conception. She's Celtic daft. She goes to all the games, compiles scrapbooks and has a video library.

'That big shite still scares me,' continues Karen, picking the crumbs off her lap. 'See when you're on the night shift . . . Yes, I know nothing's going to happen that'll involve me, but that's not the point, it's not fair. Nobody's got the right to scare me.'

'He's seen off one wife, he's got another a bag of nerves, now he's working on you.' I'm laughing but I'm not funny. I worry about Karen when I'm on the night shift. 'Don't worry yourself,' I say, 'they're in the wrong. We'll be able to do something.' I'm sounding like Mr Barraclough again.

'You don't know that, bud. Some people live their lives that way. You wonder why they ever got married in the first place. Surely to God she knew what he was like?'

'I've family like that, remember.' I say this because it's true and she knows it. 'If it's bad tonight I'll see him tomorrow and make an appointment with Jardine. Maybe do that anyway.'

'I just wish they'd fucking die.'

'I never told you the story my dad told me about him, did I?'

She shakes her head and doesn't look very interested.

'Well, my dad could tell you quite a few stories about him. Our friend is quite a local character. You'll like this one. Anyway, he was with this lassie and they'd been out at the dancing over the old town hall and were waiting for a bus at the Banana Bridge. He was well bevvied and pushing the lassie about, like – according to my dad this lassie actually went on to become his first wife – anyhow, the girl was obviously fairly upset and pretty emotional. Eh, in other words she was crying

– when along comes this wee boy and tells him to stop hitting the girl. He was only ten or eleven, like, wee guy, but, guess what, he started really laying the boot into the big shite. My dad says our friend lashed out at the wee boy and the boy ran away crying. So the bus arrives and the couple get on board. Now just as it turns down Reid Brothers Road the windscreen gets absolutely splattered with fish and chips. There's fish and chips all over the place. The driver's wondering what the fuck's going on when three guys come diving onto the bus and go storming up the back and drag our big friend off. Then they give him a right good doing and horse him in the river.

'It transpired that the wee boy was the last in line of the famous, mad, mental McClinchy family and those were his three brothers. He'd wandered off while his brothers were getting the family's fish suppers. That's how he's got that scar over his eye.'

'It's a pity they never killed him,' says Karen. She is disappointed at the lack of a gorier ending and inserts two whole Abernethys in her mouth. She likes her Abernethys, does Karen.

'It's a good story that. It's true as well. As I say, my dad could tell you quite a few about him. Mind you, that's one of the few where he was on the receiving end. My grandfather knows him as well.'

'Mmmmm. Characters should be talked about, not lived with. They should live in a part of town away from me. That's what they did in the good old days. Locked them away. Got them at birth and said "he looks a dodgy cunt" then sent them to some colony or other.' Karen brings her knees up to her chest and bites them.

'I thought women were supposed to be attracted to that type?'

'Don't talk to me about women. I don't know anything about women. I hate bloody women. They'll go out with anything. Anyway, we're different. I'm your first girlfriend and you're my first boyfriend, we've missed a lot of the shit that fucks people up.'

'Good.' I'm pleased about that. I can't believe there's a

cuddlier woman alive. I don't like to see her pissed off. 'Cheer up a bit.'

'Nah.' She bites her ankles (double-jointed). 'I get that crap at work all the time. See if I don't go in singing and dancing every day they think I'm pregnant. It's all this "what's up with you the day . . . what's up with your face . . . cheer up, hen, it'll never happen".' She does her wee wifie voices.

'Sorry.'

'I'VE GOT IT!' Karen slaps her knees with a ferocity that would shatter bricks as crumbs of Abernethy fly in every direction. 'I'll send a letter to their house and address it to Karen McClinchy. I'll get my brother to put it in one of his envelopes and post it from Glasgow.'

'I can just imagine you saying, "Oh, didn't you know my maiden name's McClinchy".'

'Oh, it's magic. Karen's a genius. I'll ever so subtly mention my uncles – or would they be my great uncles?' Karen ponders. 'I don't really wish he was dead. I wish I wish he was dead, though, know what I mean?'

'Put on *Cheers*, my mad, mental Miss McClinchy.'

Karen fires the remote as though it were a gun, and those chins appear on the screen as though firing back.

When I Heard About The Mars Bar
The Shop Was Shut

Hello, stranger.

Oh, hiya . . .

This you up for a visit?

Eh, yeah – a couple of days . . . Was round seeing Geo last night.

He never changes. The guy is cracked.

I hear congratulations are in order. When's it due?

September . . . It was planned, like. I'm not being a stupid wee lassie.

Good. You're doing all right then. I'm pleased for you.

Richard's his name. Richard Hunter. He works in the Chemicals.

I don't know the guy at all.

Mmmmm. He's from Alloa. We get on really well.

. . .

. . .

Yeah, I'm just in, eh, getting some stuff for a chilli. I'm making the tea the night. Trying to prove to my mum that I cook for myself . . . Oh, how's your folks?

Fine. Fine. How's your love life?

Oh, nothing special . . . It's amazing this. I've just realized this is the first time I've ever seen you with your natural hair colour.

Ha, I suppose it is.

Yeah . . . Eh, as I say, I haven't seen any of the gang yet. Just Geo.

We never see much of anybody. Everybody just drifted . . . You're looking well, anyway.

So are you . . . You always did.

. . .

. . .

Mmmmm. What does that mean?

You know.

Mmmmm.

Callander Park on a Summer's Day

'Would you believe those flats are like gold dust? Oh, they're forever telling us how they were wrong, how they were "inappropriate to the needs of ordinary people". Huh. They should see some of the places I go into.' Andy admired the tower blocks as though they were the pyramids themselves. He turned to his companion and added, 'Do you fancy a game of pitch-and-putt, Irene?'

'No. Let's just go to the far end and bask in the sun.'

It was the hottest day of the year. It hit you when you stopped – and Andy didn't want to stop. Irene wasn't bothered by the heat. She'd travelled the world when Mark was in the army and had grown to love it. When Mark retired, they settled in Linlithgow and Mark took up an insurance job, but died three years later. He'd always smoked and he'd always smoked a lot. Andy aged with Mark but his military career had never stretched beyond a National Service stint in Kenya, battling against the heat and the Mau-Mau. He worked as a plumber with the council. A few years till retirement yet he told folk, never giving away his age. His Lyn had died in Bellsdyke three years previous. She'd been an alcoholic. It wasn't sudden.

'You're very quiet today,' said Andy.

Irene was getting used to these kind of comments and didn't respond with anything more than a smile at Andy's unease. Their getting together had been instigated by Andy's brother who was an old customer of Mark's — Irene became a dancing partner for Andy over the Christmas and New Year festivities and things had taken their own course from there. They started out by accompanying each other on the visiting rounds. Neither had been comfortable doing this on their own, but as a couple things were easier. Mostly they talked about their children. Irene's were grown up and living away from home: an actress in London and a geologist in Aberdeen. Andy doted on his daughter, who was twenty and still lived at home. Despite the age difference, she and Irene gossiped and ganged-up like sisters, frequently at Andy's expense.

'I'm going to suffer if I stay out here too long,' said Andy rubbing his scalp.

'Stop moaning and relax,' said Irene. 'I've got plenty of lotion.'

'I suppose this weather brings back a lot of happy memories for you.'

'No. Not at all. Just the here and now.'

The heat was really starting to get to Andy. Try as he might, he just could not relax. His daughter said that he was hyper-active cause he ate too much red meat. His late wife had said he was boring. And Irene, well, he didn't know what Irene thought about him.

'I'm afraid I need the toilet,' said Andy. 'I'll only be a minute.'

'Just go in the woods.'

'I couldn't do that.' Andy pointed to the children.

'Well, don't be long then,' said Irene. 'And be careful. There's a lot of fast-moving youngsters going about.'

'I quite fancy a pair of roller-boots, actually. Do you think they'd suit me?'

'Don't be daft, you'd break your neck.'

A nice, cool hospital ward would do me fine, thought Andy, as he headed off. There was but one fluffy wee cloud in the sky and the sun raced past it in a matter of seconds making Andy grateful for the shade of the trees that lined his route.

On his way to the toilet he said 'Hello' to one of his neighbours and a couple whose house he'd been in the previous week. The neighbour had been slow to recognize Andy. Presumably because Andy was wearing shorts for the first time in years. His skinny, pale legs were starting to nip.

Andy went to the toilet just to make him feel less guilty about lying to Irene. He further purged his guilt by stopping at the shop and purchasing a couple of large cones. Irene was forever teasing him about never carrying any money on him.

Andy never felt he needed any. He never spent money on anything other than the weekly messages. He had no vices. The cost of the cones truly shocked him.

Andy walked briskly so the cones wouldn't melt too much. When he got back, though, he couldn't see Irene. He wasn't even sure he was at the right bit, it had been so long since he'd last been in the park. All he could see was unfamiliar faces wearing bright t-shirts and those stupid-looking long shorts. Andy asked some boys who were fishing if they'd seen her but they hadn't. He walked over to the woods but he couldn't see her in there either. The ice-cream was melting and running down his wrists as though, like toothpaste, he was squeezing it out. He couldn't see Irene anywhere. This was just what he didn't want. Andy threw the cones down and started crying.

'What's the matter?' Irene and her camera emerged from behind some bushes. Her joke had gone terribly wrong.

'What are you playing at?' said Andy. 'I've not got my contacts in. I can't see a blooming thing. I thought you'd gone. I wish you had now. I don't want you seeing me like this.'

'I'm sorry. It was stupid . . . But you're the one who's being stupid now.' Irene was smiling but she wasn't making a joke of it. The teasing had gone too far.

'I keep thinking, what's all this leading to? Please don't get me wrong, you make me very happy, but you've hardly said a word all day. I don't think you understand how I feel about you. There's too many question marks.'

'I wouldn't be here if I didn't want to be.'

'That's very good of you but that's not what I mean. Can we start talking about things? Things like the future?'

'Yes. I'd like that.'

'Well, Irene, I'm very lonely and I care about you a lot.'

'I feel the same way.'

'Well, what it is is . . .' Andy stopped. He was thinking about his late wife who'd always cried to get her own way. She always said she couldn't help it. That's how Andy felt just now. But it was wrong. Like telling a lie. Even though he couldn't control it.

Irene spoke for him. She said, 'I'd like to sell my house and move in with the pair of you. If that's all right.'

Andy's expression changed and the past seemed a long way away, like a holiday, not so much forgotten as finished. It was only ever a part of something. 'Oh, boy', he said. 'Well . . . eh . . . we'll . . . we'll need to . . .' He couldn't think of what to say. He looked at the cones and that focused his thoughts. 'Do you know how much those blooming things cost, by the way?'

Irene laughed and picked up the cones. She smiled at Andy and planted them on his freckly scalp, for all the world making him look like a playschool devil, but feeling inside like a real, live angel.

Life on a Scottish Council Estate
Vol. I Chap. I

. . . and I'm playing some records and dancing about and generally enjoying myself when there's a knock at the door. It's Wee Harry and his problems. He tells me Wendy's chucked him so I let him in and make him a coffee and prepare to hear his life story for the millionth time. Just as we reach the part where his mam used to serenade him with 'Nobody loves you/ you're nobody's child', Edwyn and English Edgar arrive. Edwyn skins up and English Edgar says my flat's fair stinking of oranges and Marlboro. Just like California, I tell him. We take our cue and slap on some Beach Boys records. Wee Harry feels we're ignoring him (which we are) so him and his problems take their leave. The Tank is next to appear. He's got a few cans and joins us singing along to 'California Girls'. Edwyn and English Edgar depart when the dope and the bevvy run out . . . The Tank dives into my records . . . He comes out with The Stones, Cheap Trick, Alice Cooper and Guns 'n' Roses (the closest I've got to AC/DC). We get out the golf clubs and mime guitar solos and use them as microphones. The Tank says 'Is that the door?' And it is. It's Stuart this time. Stuart is looking for Edwyn and English Edgar cause he heard they had a bit of dope. We tell him that they were here but that they left when the dope and the bevvy ran out . . . Stuart is distraught . . . He skins up the roaches while wondering aloud who would be prepared to sell him hash on tick. This is difficult since Stuart owes money to everybody. Stuart is a divorced psychiatric nurse in real life. The Tank pisses off cause he can't stand Stuart . . . Stuart gives it the really paranoid bit about how nobody likes him. This is true. Nobody does like him. There is a knock at the door. I look out. There's no one there. I look down. Ah, it's the kids (Aaron, Jason, Abigail and Veronique) and a dog called Bongo. They come in and head

straight for my Scalectrix. Stuart makes up his mind to go and
says he's off to Steve and Sara's. They've always got hash and
he only owes them a fiver. I make myself a coffee and play
Scalectrix with the kids and a dog called Bongo. I soon
discover that Stuart has taken my full box of matches and left
his empty one. Shit! I look out the window to see if the ice-
cream van is there. It is. This is my daily exercise. I go bombing
down the stairs and out the front door. AAAAAAAAAAAAA
AAAAHHHHHHHHHHHHHHHHHHHHHHHHHHHH!! I
scream for my dear life and leap ten feet in the air as the biggest
fucking Alsatian you have ever seen leaps out from our bundle
of bin-bags . . . I compose myself and see that the Alsatian
belongs to two guys with baseball bats and balaclavas who are
presently engaged in smashing to bits a car belonging to one of
my neighbours. They ask me if I've got a problem. I say 'Nnnn-
nnnn-nn-no' and shrug my shoulders and try to look really
uninterested. When I reach the ice-cream van, however, I say
to Total Trevor – the English ice-cream man – 'Did you see
that?' He shakes his head, does his Manuel and goes 'I know
nuuuuu-ting.' Typical. So I get my matches and a snowball, a
Mars bar, a packet of McCoys, a coconut Boost, a packet of
white Buttons and a ten pence mixture. I also get ten pence
mixtures for each of the kids and a dog called Bongo. (See if I'd
have given as much money to charity as I have to the ice-cream
van, I'd have shaken hands with Princess Anne by now.) Back
at my flat I make myself another coffee and demolish my
munchies . . . I am bloated. The door goes. It's Wendy. She tells
me Wee Harry's chucked her. The kids say 'Ahhhh' as Wendy
cries and I try to comfort her. The kids and a dog called Bongo
can't stand the slushy bits so they decide to leave. They remind
me I've got an all-night babysitting session on Friday and
depart to plot my downfall. I return to Wendy. I put on this
specially compiled Prince tape I made up for comforting
distressed women . . . It works and before the end of
'Condition of the Heart' she's going, 'Gordon! Gordon! I want
to have your babies' and we're partying like crazy through in
my spare bedroom . . . In the afterglow there's a knock at the
door. *Oh, no, it's my psychotic big brother!* My psychotic big

brother drinks Newcastle Brown to make him violent and whisky to make him maudlin. Wendy departs screaming as my psychotic big brother batters fuck out of me and says sorry at the same time . . . After he's finished with me, I wash myself and nurse my injuries whereupon Hamish arrives and offers to sell me records I've already got. He says, 'They're really cheap, but.' He then tries to sell me a camera. Grant puts in an appearance. Grant comes round on the off-chance of bumping into Wee Harry. He wishes to befriend Wee Harry and gain a subsequent introduction to Wee Harry's wee sister, for whom he carries a horn of almost Alpine proportions . . . Grant circles my living-room . . . He offers me a fag. He makes polite conversation for three seconds . . . Then he says, 'Seen Wee Harry recently?' I say he's been and gone. Grant gets up and leaves. (He's pretty serious about this wee lassie.) Hamish chases after him shouting, 'Do you want to buy a camera? Do you want to buy a camera?' I make myself a coffee but before I reach the comfort of my settee the door goes again. It's my pal Mikey. He's just up from London and heads straight for my records. He selects Steely Dan's *Countdown to Ecstasy* (he's dead nostalgic when he gets back to my bit) and we mime all the solos and remember all the words. Then we have a singles battle. We each seek out a record and defy the other to find a better one. This ends up with us arguing and damned near falling out. My pal Mikey says, 'I recognize that knock — IT'S THE BIG MAN!' And it is. The Big Man is an airline pilot in real life. (You think I'm joking!) He earns £30,000 a year, wears ludicrous Noel Edmunds jackets and is just back from Mexico. He's got a massive carry-out, a carrier-bagful of munchies and a bit of dope the size of Gibraltar. 'You know how those old Mexican geezers look completely out of it?' he says with a megagrin on his face. Me and my pal Mikey say 'Ye-essss.' 'Well,' says The Big Man, 'this is the stuff that does it.' Me, my pal Mikey and The Big Man get stuck into the bevvy and the munchies and investigate the dope . . . We are soon looking like old Mexican geezers. My pal Mikey says he can't feel his legs or his eyelids. He crashes out in my spare bedroom. Me, I don't feel too good. For the first time in my life, I fail to finish off munchies. I tell The Big Man just to crash out in my living-room. He looks pleased with himself, now that he's turned us into zombies, and says he's just going to roll himself a single-skinner to ease him off to sleep. History has told me that he only managed to smoke half of it before achieving the desired state. Leaving the other half to start a fire which would in turn burn my fucking flat down.

That's What It's Like to be Grown-up

Only my dad could fix us up with this shithole. I mean, the bed's held thegether with sellotape and there's not even a lightshade. It's like Colditz, man. You can't sleep for cats and dogs and rattling windows, the water tastes like it's gone off and see the food . . . Christ, I spend most of my time in here. I hate it. I hate holidays. I hate England. Hey, what's that rubbed into that wall? . . . It's shit! No, surely no . . . God, it is. *God, it's shit, man!* That does it. I'm never going on holiday with them again. Ever. My dad never even got me a room of my own. Says he requested one when he booked up. Lying, stingy bastard. I'm never forgiving him. No, no more family holidays for me. Christ, my sister'll be having a great time. Greyyyy-hummmm'll be there. Getting drunk and having parties. She'll be her little Miss Innocent when we get back, though. Just you wait and see.

She's going to Scarborough with that Rachel Young – her with the big tits. I wish I was grown up. Like when I was showing Clare how to work that camera and – ohhhh – I had my arms around her, and I was rubbing my chin on her beautiful bare shoulder. Oh, those little white hairs. I could have stayed there forever, man. That's what it's like to be grown-up.

She's got a room to herself, Clare has. They're leaving tomorrow though. Going somewhere else. Clare's special. I've got to try and swap addresses. Got to. See when she was telling me about her sunburn – man, I thought I was going to explode. Ohhh.

Still half an hour till the Zaire game. We're going to destroy them like we did with Cyprus. We're going to draw with Brazil and then beat Yugoslavia. In the final it'll be us against Brazil again and we'll prove once and for all who's the greatest team in the world – us. We're going to win! We're going to win! We're going to win! Clare'll be there. She's supporting Scotland.

Ohhhh Clare. Ohhhh Clare. Ohhhh Clare.

I've got to go out and get myself something that's going to remind me of Clare. Got to. Something that'll be everlasting. Something special. I know what I'll do. I'll buy an LP. My first ever LP. One that's going to remind me of Clare and one that's going to last for all time. There's no doubt about it, it's got to be – Nazareth's *Razamanaz*. Dan McCafferty is God. My sister wouldn't let me go and see them. Just cause Greyyyy-hummmm was there. I really hate him, man. Can't stand him. When we all went to the baths at Easter he tried to drown me so I pissed all over his clothes when we got back to the changing-rooms.

Oh, I hope that woman's at her window over the back the night. *Whoooa-ahhhh*. She takes her clothes off, man! Last night she just had a bra on. And then the football starts and I have to go downstairs. That is the moment she takes her bra off. *Bddd-umph. Ohhhh*.

'Clare, are you in the toilet?'

Oh no, my dad's going to batter me! She's trying to get in. Christ, the door's not locked right! Quick! . . . Boy, that was close.

'That is you, isn't it? . . . Come on, dear, I just want a word with you.'

What about, like?

'Sulking in the toilet won't do you any good . . . Look, it's time to have a serious talk about things.'

Heh heh.

'Clare – you're making a fool of yourself. It's as simple and straightforward as that . . . It was just a holiday crush. Nothing more. And he . . . well, he was just using you.'

For God's sake, missus, I didn't use her. All I did was put my arms around her and rub my chin against her shoulder. *Ohhhh*. Don't talk about us like that. I love her.

'It's finished, Clare. You'll never see him again and believe me it's for the best . . . He wasn't really nice, was he?'

Get stuffed! Snobby bitch!

'Look . . . I understand these things. Probably a lot better than you'd give me credit for. I was young once myself. I've had experience of his type before.'

His type?

'You're just a very young girl, Clare. Listen . . . Brian is not for you.'

BRIAN!

'He's nineteen, Clare.'

NINETEEN!

'Mum, what are you doing?'

TWO-TIMING!

'Ah, Clare . . . Eh, where have you been?'

BAS-TARD!

'Getting a newspaper for Dad.'

SH-ITE!

'Then who's . . .'

PISS *OFF*!

'What?'

GO A-*WAY*!

'Never mind. Let's go and find your father. He'll be wanting to watch the football.'

What . . . but . . . why . . . how . . . huh. *Bastard!* I bet he looks like Greyyyy-hummmm or Dan McCafferty.

'Stoorie Will, are you in there?'

'Yes, mum.'

'What a brasser that wife got when her lassie appeared. You should've seen her. Me and your dad nearly wet ourselves. Anyway, how's the bowels doing? . . . Well, come on then. I've got your scarf. SCOT-LAND!'

The Sixties

I remember the lorries going up and down our street. I remember the outside toilet and the metal bath. I remember my dad on the railways and my mum beating carpets. I remember our first car and the door that fell off. I remember the smells of petrol and diesel and beaches and fields. I remember a really brilliant game of football being stopped cause we had to go in and watch some arseholes walking on the moon. I remember an orange shirt and an orange tie. I remember Mrs Spiller's mini . . . and what we did to Debbie Brown at the bowling club. I remember my first girlfriend moving to Stenhousemuir and my second moving to Australia. I remember seeing starving children on television. But I remember being picked for my first proper team. And I remember scoring my first goal with real nets. A twelve-yard volley it was.

Career Opportunities

Although they all expected the foreman's job would be offered to him, Charlie never let on that he'd already been invited to take up the post. As he watched the news and drank his tea, Charlie mulled over the proposal.

The position had arisen following the death of Charlie's pal, Frazer Doyle. As the workforce had streamlined and the day-to-day duties became more diverse and more involved, Frazer's health and well-being could be said to have suffered accordingly. Frazer was always the ambitious one, but he was also the anxious one. The butt of many a prank, he maintained a good relationship with the men but latterly his ability to get on with the bosses was strained. Like the policemen, they just got younger and younger.

Michael and Steven represented the new breed of boss. Itinerant management brought in to liaise with others as much as to look after their own. Michael was selfish, highly strung and prone to bouts of paranoid hysteria. Steven, on the other hand, worked away in virtual solitude, compiling files and files of 'programmes' and 'packages', pertaining to what, no one really gave an earthly. The men christened them 'The Blasé Cunts'. But they could talk alright. Boy, could they talk. They never lost arguments cause they never shut up. Inevitably, Michael would get hysterical and Steven would show you his paperwork.

Charlie had been brought up by elderly grandparents and moved away from the small community as soon as he could. On his first day at his new job in, what was for him, the big city, Charlie met, and was befriended by, Frazer. Frazer was not so much older as wiser, his ambition fuelled as much by responsibility as personal gain. Charlie and Frazer had remained close friends ever since. Through knowing Frazer's wife and daughter, Charlie experienced not only grief and loss, but a sense of mortality of which he'd previously been ignorant: a sense of good fortune and the passing of time, what insurance meant and why people made wills. For the first time since his childhood, he'd even thought about God.

The funeral had brought together the old shift: a nine-man team that made Bilko's motorpool look like a masterclass in elegance and diligence. Some of them Charlie hadn't seen for ages, but they'd all turned up. Charlie supped his tea as he reminisced. There was Big Malcolm who earned more money doing building work on the side than he ever did from the company; Raymond 'Victor' Davies, nicknamed after his lookalike, the giraffe that died; Polish Jacki and his strange grasp of English; Trainer Steve Lawson, forever boasting about his extra-marital girlfriends until the day he went home to discover his wife and the two kids had moved in with the insurance man – this didn't bother him too much but she'd smashed his train set to bits and the poor lad was inconsolable; Paul Mazio, whose life Frazer had saved when they had that fire back in '74; Wee Kevin and his fickle eating habits; Willie Brown – the token nutter, *the total nutter*. 'Member the time he fell asleep on the top of a tree on that fishing trip, Charlie thought to himself. Jesus, what a weekend that was.

These people were Charlie's first family really. He responded to them and introduced his wife to them as though they were family. Charlie was bitter his sons hadn't experienced this part of growing up – being forced to get on with people not of your choosing – but seemed content just to laze about the house, mixing with ne'er-do-wells and getting involved in God-knows-what. Maybe, Charlie thought, he should have been harder on them. Occasionally things would erupt into major rows, stemming not so much from antagonism but from the frustration felt by both sides. Charlie had enjoyed a wild spell in his youth, but his sons didn't even seem capable of that. The worry they caused their mother sometimes got to him.

At the work, Charlie had watched the old shift dwindle down to just three men. Sure, there probably was a time when they were overmanned and underefficient, but things had been better then. More enjoyable. It was an easier life, less demanding. Now things were worse and things were different. It was all small firms with no unions. Just work, work, work. Charlie laughed to himself as he supposed that's what it was always supposed to be . . . dull.

It was with all this in mind that Charlie considered the offer. If the company brought in a new man they'd have to pay for his training, and even then they were only going to get a Michael or a Steven. The previous year they had offered Charlie early retirement, now they offered him promotion, not because he was exceptional but because he was suitable. This wasn't a reward for merit, this was 'you'll do'.

Before the football came on, Charlie phoned up the work and left a message on the office answering-machine saying he declined the offer.

Nine of Us

That's what this job is, responsibility. Something gets broken, I'm responsible. Something goes missing, I'm responsible. I'm responsible for seeing they've got work to do, and I'm responsible for monitoring said work. If it was proper wages I could at least present the illusion of authority. If it was proper work I wouldn't spend most of my time thinking about what to do next.

I call them 'The Customers': the customer is always right; the customer is passing through; I am here to serve the customer. The people who pay my wages gave me ten pages of guidelines, twelve books of background and one piece of advice – don't get involved.

The younger ones have got CVs made up of programmes, projects and what we call periods of voluntary study. The older ones are surplus tradesmen and factory women. I like them a lot. See when they're feeding off each other, going on about football and families, and sex and telly, they hold back nothing. Nothing's forbidden, nothing's too personal. I'm not prone to doing an Esther Rantzen but some of this lot's experiences have left me a little choked. You don't get nutters coming here, it's the shy ones and the victims.

Now Dave's as academically smart as anyone I've met but he just won't work. He sees humour in everything, the ridiculous in everything. He can't do anything without laughing. The bulk of Dave's humour is directed at Willie and Tam. Willie and Tam take offence at advice and umbrage at instruction, yet they'll do whatever I ask of them. 'Shift this . . . move that' and they'll do it. Sure, they'll question the purpose and take ten times longer than they should but they'll do *anything*! Kate, on the other hand, says and does next to nothing. Ask her a question and the response is a shrug or a 'What?' or a 'Don't know'. Tricia tells me it's boyfriend trouble. Tricia's old enough to be my mother and unofficially runs this place. Despite the range of exotic t-shirts she wears, she's lived in this town all her life and hardly ever been out of it; admitting to having been to Edinburgh once and England twice. She has a good word to say about neither. The doctor told her to quit smoking and stop drinking coffee. She told him he'd be as well right there and then to put a rope around her neck and cut her throat. The t-shirts come from her family; of whom I've heard so much I know them better than my own. When Steve arrived he was quiet and cagey about himself. Willie, Tam and Dave parodied him thus: Willie or Tam would say, 'Nice weather, Steve/How you doing, Steve?/See the Arsenal did well on Saturday, Steve/See World War III's started, Steve, etc.' and Dave would brilliantly take off Steve's wary demeanour and Glasgow accent, saying, 'Oh, I don't want to talk about it and that, you know'. Tricia, however, felt that Steve's awkwardness was more easily explained. 'The poor lad's a boring bastard,' she said. This place has been good for Steve, though. He's been writing off for jobs and even had a couple of interviews. As has Peter, our resident gloom and doom merchant. A party political broadcast on behalf of the miserable shits, he's got a wife, five kids and an index finger permanently homed in on me. I spend a lot of my time helping him out with his entitlements. It's hellish the shit he has to go through. Used to be a woman in here lost out on free school meals for her kids cause she was 40p above the threshold.

I'm here because this is the lowest rung on the middle-management ladder. I started my own business and it failed – as did my marriage. Like everyone else I just came here to put something on my CV to show prospective employers I wasn't sitting about doing nothing.

Not so long ago I was applying for several jobs a week, now I don't bother. I'm enjoying this. I like the in-jokes and the fun of it. I just wished they all got the same money as me, that's all. (Six thousand a year, by the way. A modest salary, to be sure.) This wee bit of guilt encourages me to play the nice guy round here. I pay for the tea and coffee and spend a couple of quid a week on biscuits. I'm not supposed to do things like that.

It's been a difficult time for me recently, what with the divorce and all, and it's been good to have people like Tricia I can talk to about things, and Dave who thinks it's all hilarious. As he puts it, 'Did she find somebody with a decent-sized cock then or what?' Many a true word spoken by an irritating shit.

So why do people come here? I mean, there's no money in it. What extra money they do get goes on fish-supper dinners and endless cans of Coke. Some of them take two buses to get here. Why bother? It's cause it's what they've been used to. They've never had money: money to do things, money to buy things, money to fuck up and money to fall back on. They've only known money as something to exist by. A decent job is viewed with the same level of prospect as winning the pools. And, as I said, I like them, they like each other too. We've had romances in here. I take great pride in the fact that we invented the monkey and the wardrobe jokes. *It was us.* And if home is as bad as they say it is, then this will be better: talking, joking, meeting new friends, having a riot. One of the posters proclaims 'Anything that gets you out of the house is good'. Underneath someone (Dave) has written 'If work's so good, how come you want to go back to sleep when you wake up in the morning?'. Below this someone (Tricia) has added, 'If life's so good, how come you want to go back to sleep when you wake up in the morning?'.

I'm never sure what's best for them. Whether I should 'help' them or just let them enjoy themselves. I favour the former cause it gives me something to do, and it's what I'm paid for, I suppose. Part of the 'training' here involves me giving them confidence-building exercises. One week I got them to compose and deliver speeches about themselves. The content was good but the presentation was, well — shite. Tricia was away seeing her doctor again so the whole thing got a bit out of control. Willie and Tam said, that's it, and that they weren't coming back. True to form, though, they did return, moaning as usual. The following week I got them just to write the things down and said I would deliver the speeches. So it no longer became an exercise for them but an indulgence for me. Dave refused to tell us about himself and instead envisaged a scenario wherein The Fat Slags (of Viz comics – our bible) joined our team and paired off with Willie and Tam. Kate's concerned a holiday she and her boyfriend had gone on at the end of last year. It was flat and a little dull – like the weather she constantly referred to – but it was sincere and believable. Willie and Tam went to the trouble of copying something out of a porn mag. It must've taken them hours. Steve's was the shocker. The previous week we'd packed in before we got round to him so I don't know if it was what he had originally intended doing. It was about how he'd been mugged a few months ago and ended up in intensive care. He went on to detail the trouble he'd had in getting compensation and the pathetic sentences his attackers had received. Since then, Steve has never stopped going on about it. He doesn't get much sympathy from round here. Willie, Tam and Dave have modified the sketch: the same introduction with Dave then alternating between describing the attack, the hospital or the court case. 'I hate folk like that,' says Dave. 'They're a pain. Don't deny it.' Dave can come away with some crackers. He's a bit dodgy at times.

We let Peter off cause he's got reading and writing difficulties. Tricia's was amazing. She delivered it herself. She described with undue innocence all the times in the last twelve months when she had tried to kill her husband. She'd tried poison, tampering with his brakes and assault, but 'the bastard just would not die'.

I said there were nine of us. There's The Big Man, Big Alan. The only one here you'd call brash, he's eighteen stone and Celtic daft. On his first day he brought in a hammer. Perplexed, I ask him why. He looked at me as if I knew nothing about nothing and said, 'There'll be a use for it. There always is.' Time proved him right, of course. We've also to thank him for supplying industrial tape, a screwdriver, a radio, a kettle, a heater and a football – all courtesy of his car boot. With incontestable logic he stores everything there cause it's always handy and easy to find. Monday mornings are the best. Alan comes in and regales us till elevenses with all the jokes he's heard over the weekend. He drinks the weakest tea I've ever seen and he's the funniest guy I know.

Alan's suffered from heart trouble and was using this place as a stepping-stone to getting back to real work. He was really keen so I got him a work-replacement with a firm up the road, doing some fork-lifting a couple of days a week.

It's a quarter to four on a Tuesday and I've just had a phone call saying there's been an accident, Alan's been injured and taken to hospital. Now I've got to make twenty phone calls and everyone in this office is staring at me, knowing something's wrong. As I said, my job's responsibility – and I'm never allowed to forget it.

A Blues

She tells me she has three kids and that her husband's in prison. She doesn't seem too bothered. She sounds like she means it when she says he could be dead for all she cared.

She doesn't talk fast but she doesn't need to. I'm not the interrupting type. She says my name when she speaks. She's friendly. She's not a stupid wee lassie.

I didn't want any of this. I just went down the pub to make sure Doc was getting my ticket for Saturday. There was a gang of them and she was there. She was a bit drunk when I arrived and she's what you'd call merry now. We're back at my flat. I've made the coffee and she's sitting beside my electric fire, her hands caressing the imitation coal. She put the fire on.

I never knew about the kids or the husband. I hardly know her at all, really. She was just that lassie that used to work behind the bar. I think Alec fancied her. I could have guessed about the kids, mind you. There's a standing joke with our lot about the pregnant barmaids.

She isn't feeling sorry for herself. She takes an interest in what I say. Occasionally she stops and I remember how drunk she is. I get worried she's going to cry or be sick or fall asleep or something. She gets up from the fire and I can see that two middle buttons on her shirt are undone and the zip at the back of her skirt is halfway down.

She planks herself on my settee and invariably we get round to talking about school. I work out she's the same age as my sister. We talk further then remembering each other. We all went to a disco once. I had glitter round my eyes and she wore a tartan waistcoat. They were good times. I fill her in about my sister then I ask about her husband. I don't know him but she's sure I'd recognize him. He was a mistake, she says. She tells me how he got arrested for armed-with-a-penknife robbery, and how he made pots of tea in the middle of the night as an apology for being hopeless in bed. Only one of the kids is his, she confides; though not I suspect for the first time.

I ask about the kids. She tells me they're with her mother. Her mother left her father and moved in with them at the start of the year . . . Her father beat her mother . . . Her expression is anxious as though bad memories are threatening to take over. She collects herself and tells me one day they stole half his furniture while he was out at work.

She laughs and says the female side of her family are all thieves. She tells me about the time she 'borrowed' keycards from an ex-boyfriend and emptied his accounts. She says that to this day he has no idea it was her who did it – and she still has his doorkey so she could do it again.

She starts slagging me. She's teasing and I tell her so. She says all women tease. The room is boiling and I'm very tired. That tired I know I won't sleep. She asks if I'm religious. I shake my head. She shakes hers in disappointment. She starts talking about God. She goes to church and her faith is strong. Her faith in God.

I tell her I have work in the morning. She tells me so does she but that one of the kids has to go to the health centre and they need her signature, so she'll get a lie-in and the morning off. Her mum sees to the kids at breakfast time.

She asks what I'm thinking about. I get a bit flustered. She says she just said that to make me blush. She adopts a West Indian accent and says, 'I like to see white people blush.' I laugh and tell her I think mostly about my work.

She relaxes and looks peaceful. Like she's had a big meal or a long journey . . . or too much to drink. I can hear her breathing. She declares that she is drunk. I nod and nick one of her cheeky faces to show that I'd noticed.

I go to the toilet. I hate myself for thinking she might be stealing something. When I return she's kneeling by my records. The zip on her skirt is all the way down allowing a bulge of underwear to jut out. She slags my records and asks if I've got any Bryan Adams. *No.* She gets up and falls flat back onto my settee. I can see her sweaty armpits as she flings her arms back.

I ask if she's taking the kids on holiday. This dumbfounds her. She tells me how much it costs to look after the kids, not forgetting her mother. No matter how much she makes it all goes on the kids. She says that she has great battles with the kids – and that she always wins. She blows on her fingertips and brushes her chest. It all sounds like work because it is work, she says.

She asks if I'm still hung up on Frances. I tell her that situation's a bit up in the air at the moment. I'm surprised she knew about me. I think she'll know a lot about a lot of people. She tells me never to marry or live with anyone. She says she made the same mistake twice.

She says she has to go. I'm glad. I tell her it's because I've only got two fags left. She gives me hers and says it's okay cause she'll nick her mam's. The thief smiles. She stands at my window and slags off this town. I knew that was coming and tell her so. She smiles again and asks if Doc had my ticket. Yeah, sort of. She says that when she gets home she will kneel by the beds of her children and pray. She tells me that she prays every night and that her prayers come true. I ask what she prays for. She prays for the children: for their health and their future. She says nobody'll take her with three kids but she doesn't care. She says that she'd go through everything again just to have the children. She says she'll mention me in her prayers.

I offer to see her home. She says it's all right. She just lives in the next court. The flat with the purple curtains. Every room has purple curtains. I tell her I don't notice things like that.

She thanks me for the coffee and apologizes for being a pain in the bum. She looks attractive now. Her skin is soft and her eyes are alert. She lets herself out into the close and the smell of booze, fags and heat gives way to a freshness. I tell her to take care of herself . . . and her kids . . . and her mam. She points to her flat. The light's still on. She laughs and says the stupid old bitch is still waiting up for her.

Wee Man

It never occurred to me you might get hurt. You're all I've got. There was no need for it. I've devoted the last six years of my life to you: being amused by you, being frightened by you and being really pissed off. Why does it always have to be a battle? Must you always wind me up?

One roll, that's what I've had today. One roll. I forget what was in it. I forget what happened today. Something to do with Carla. I'm picking you up then I'm going straight to my bed. Don't care if it's only half-seven.

I'm the only person he can treat like this. He thinks he's fly. 'Stop 'menting me, mam. Stop 'menting me.' Oh, will you please be quiet? Will you please do as you're told? Look, don't start. Don't make me hit you again.

Tangible

It had been an encouraging morning at the council and the training centre and May afforded herself a little optimism upon seeing the first daffodils of the year.

Good. This'll shorten the winter. Every day like this shortens the winter.

May had been complaining to the council about the state of the pavements, the rubbish in her garden and the noise the kids made at night.

The pavements were a disgrace: a mixture of dangerous cracked flagstones and irregular surfaces potholed to such an extent that even after a shower May had to walk on the road to avoid the puddles. It was treacherous, May told Mrs Bell at the council. She told Mrs Bell how she'd heard on the radio that two hundred people every year died as a result of injuries sustained on Britain's pavements. Mrs Bell, who'd remembered May's name from last week, was sympathetic and agreed something ought to be done about it, but she went on about subsidence and designers and contractors and said nothing could be started until next year, at the earliest.

May's house was next to a chippie and a late-night grocer's. The kids from school went there at dinner time and hung about there at nights, shouting and screaming then chucking their crisp packets and cans into her garden. What she really wanted, May told Mrs Bell, was one of those new one-bedroomed flats over the town – where Isa lived – and away from kids and schools and shops. May said her arthritis had been playing up and she couldn't look after the garden. (A white lie – her arthritis hadn't been troubling her of late, touch wood.) Mrs Bell asked if there was anyone who could look after the garden for her. No, May said, the family had gone and the neighbours' gardens were in a worse state than hers. (The truth.) May had got ruffled when Mrs Bell said the

Tenants' Association kept a list of volunteers who would do gardening work for her. May said she didn't like that lot, and wanted nothing to do with them. It was a transfer she wanted, she was desperate for one. Mrs Bell said she understood and told May she would get extra points if she brought in a doctor's line about the arthritis; but that she still wouldn't have enough to get into the new flats.

This was the third week in a row May had been in with the same complaints. She was running out of things to say and just stood there, anxious and despondent. Mrs Bell was aware of this and, after a second, said she'd been looking through the records and had seen that May's house was among the next batch to be renovated. She said that they didn't like decanting elderly people and maybe it would be best all round if May was to be relocated permanently. Mrs Bell said she would see what she could do but that she couldn't promise anything. In the meantime she told May she should badger her councillor at the Saturday morning surgeries. Mrs Bell checked to see no one could overhear and added in a whisper that 'rules would require to be bent'. Her nose-touching gesture and her friendly expression had been encouraging.

There's young Sharon. Look at the figure on her! What a waistline she's got!

It wasn't just the kids who were responsible for littering May's garden. There were leaflets, beer cans and whisky bottles trapped within the long grass and against the galvanized steel fence. It was a mess. The whole street was a mess and so was the estate – known locally as Calcutta. Despite constant renovations and upgrading, the area held onto its bad reputation. The Tenants' Association with its community flat provided cheap food, free advice and somewhere to go. They staged commmunity events and held annual arts festivals. May had written to the local paper complaining about the amount of money that was spent on the place.

Jobs for the boys. They'd do better to bring back the birch and ban sweets. It's not the kids. It's the parents. They don't pick up language like that from school; they get it from the parents.

For dinner, May had herself a beef-and-tomato cup-a-soup
and two slices of buttered toast. She had told the woman at the
training centre she wanted to get back to work to shorten the
days and to get her out of the house. The woman at the training
centre, Julie her name was, said these were good 'tangible'
reasons for coming to see her. They talked about May's
background in caring and Julie suggested part-time or
voluntary work. May turned her nose up at voluntary work
and Julie asked if money was really that important. May
thought for a second and said she supposed it wasn't really.
Julie gave her handouts and leaflets dealing with crêches and
nurseries, and made a proper appointment for May to come
back the following week. Julie said the rewards for voluntary
work were more 'tangible' in terms of personal satisfaction.
May looked the word 'tangible' up in the dictionary.

*You learn something every day. Why couldn't she have just
said that? I suppose she's right. I'd still have time for my
bowling. That lassie was a bit abrupt though, mind you.
Couldn't wait to get rid of me. Still, I'll see her next week. She
says she'll get me sorted out. I don't know about this child-
minding lark, looking after babies. You never know, though.*

The family hadn't phoned this year. As usual, May had
phoned at Christmas but she'd also phoned at New Year when
it was normally them that phoned. They were always busy
these days. May decided she would phone next week and see
if she could go through for the wee boy's birthday on
Valentine's Day.

*Him and his 'total trendy'. The white Mark Walters. If he
thinks he's getting that £30 sweatshirt he's got another think
coming. What else did Myra say? An AC Milan top. Where the
blazes am I supposed to get an AC Milan top?*

May checked the paper to see what was on the telly the
night. Monday was a free night. Tuesday was the wee bingo,
Wednesday was the WRI, Thursday she went to Jean and
Bob's and on Fridays she sometimes went to the big bingo. The
weekends she left free in case the family wanted to come
through. (Something that hadn't happened for ages. Although
if they said they were coming May would stall all notions of

moving.) May had got into the habit of going to church on Sundays; sometimes both services. During the days she went shopping and there was the bowls in the summer. When she was doing the housework May liked to have some tapes or the radio on. There was always housework to be seen to.

Take The High Road . . . The Krypton Factor . . . Coronation Street . . . Telly's rubbish. There's ironing needing done. I'll do that later. I better phone Helen and make an appointment for my hair if I'm going through. My feet could do with a wash after all that walking.

May took the dishes back to the kitchen and returned with a cup of tea and the last Caramel Log. She thought about going out later for some more biscuits but decided against it. She could do with losing a bit of weight and it wasn't as if she was expecting visitors.

May turned on the television and got herself comfortable. It was the wee boy who'd got her into watching *Neighbours*. Him and his pals used to come round after they'd been out playing football. May would give them juice and they'd sit round and watch the programme. She didn't see as much of him now the family had moved. When she spoke to him on the phone it gave them something else to talk about. It was more interesting than school, they agreed. They hadn't spoken as much on the phone the last time. He had himself a girlfriend these days and was going out. He'd been anxious about his date and even asked May's advice. Some things never change. May had laughed at him. He was growing up and like Henry, Joe, Jane, Sharon, Todd and little Katie, he needed all the help he could get.

Oh, I suppose he's worth a £30 sweatshirt. Saves all the hassle of looking for something, anyway. I'll get him the Kylie Minogue record as well. I better not. I think he just fancies her. Skinny wee thing.

Real Cool Cunt, A Mickey Mouse Bastard

She's late. It'll be the family's fault.

I really like her. She's too young, I suppose – four sugars in the coffee – but she's great company, natural and unpredictable. Like when she pops round after college for a few minutes. I like that. There's a factory somewhere produces these 'interesting' wee lassies with their small tits, squint noses, plukey foreheads and always asking questions – I should take out shares really. She's going through her black phase at the moment: everything she wears is slimming and mysterious black. Insecure. She tells me I'm only her third proper boyfriend. And me, well, I've been checking out this production line for years.

Gonna ask her pal and see if she'll go out with me? . . . *She says to walk past her flat at half-seven so she can see what you look like* . . . Gonna phone her for me? . . . *She says she'll meet you at the Banana Bridge at eight* . . . Do you fancy going to the ice-rink on Saturday? . . . *Mmmaybe. Give us a phone after Crossroads* . . . Are you going to Sam's party? . . . *Maybe. Give us a phone after Blockbusters* . . . Do you fancy going out for a drink sometime? . . . *Maybe. Give us a phone after Neighbours.*

And I did. And it's been all right.

So me and a couple of fat lassies are waiting outside John Menzies at the bus station. Watching all the wee kids coming in. The casuals off the buses and the neds in their cars. Coming in to get drunk, get stupid and hopefully get laid. The wee lassies with their mini-skirts, yesterday's hair-do and a developing habit for Embassy Regal. The wee boys with their designer gear, yesterday's short-back-and-sides ('don't touch the top') and a developing habit for getting wrecked. Bound for discos where the door policy amounts to looking old enough to have had your first period or for your balls to have dropped. Trouble with the police and they get a hundred lines. Slight exaggeration. Trouble with each other means taxis then hospital.

There's been a fair bit of trouble recently. More than I've seen for a while. More weapons. More gangs. More casuals, neds and nutters. The police took a doing last week outside Trax. It didn't make the papers. We're not going there.

We're going to the pictures. I love the pictures on a Saturday night. I can get really into it. I love the way those guys laugh at adverts they must have seen a million times before. I love the silence and the screaming you get during thrillers and horrors. I love the way you get the booing if things get pretentious or corny. You're together with someone but you're also in company. When you leave you can find out what's happening for the rest of the night . . . I wonder what will happen tonight.

More revellers coming in. The older ones, half a dozen to a car. Jacketless lads, a bit beefy and a bit dodgy, showing off in cars that can do nought-to-bloody-dangerous by the end of the car park. And skirt-suited lassies, either too skinny or too fat but always too loud and always smoking. I recognize one of this lot. She's been going to the same disco for the past fifteen years. Check the legs on it, man. What a mess. I wonder if I look that bad. No. No, I don't look bad at all. I'm in better shape than any of this lot.

Ah, here she comes. A number one smile. She looks exactly as she is. Friendly and popular. She's got brothers, sisters and a full complement of grandparents. She's got college, she's got friends and she goes out. I sometimes feel guilty about how I know so much about her. It's as if I've been spying. It's not. It's just that she's so open, I guess.

Well, ladies. I'm afraid I'll have to leave you, my date has arrived. I hope yours will . . . although from the look of you, I wouldn't hold out much hope.

'Hiya. Sorry I'm late. Listen, it was my dad's fault. We took a run up to see the new caravan and . . .'

Suzanne quickly explained away her lateness then went on to say she wouldn't be able to go to the pictures. It was her pal's sister's twenty-first and they had booked up to go to a restaurant. She'd forgotten all about it.

'Is that all right?' said Suzanne.

Bobby was a little disappointed but said, 'Yeah. Sure. Of course it is.'

'Do you want to meet up with us later on? We're going to Trax.'

'Eh . . . no. Not really.' Bobby didn't like Trax. Too many neds went there. Too many of his exs as well.

'Are you sure?'

'Yeah,' Bobby laughed. 'I'm a bit old for the Trax crowd. Look, have you got time to go for a drink?'

'A-ha.' Suzanne checked her watch. 'I said I would be there at half-nine . . . Look, Bobby, I'm sorry this is such short notice. I completely forgot about the birthday and everything. I've been run off my feet for the past two days. Me and Diane spent all yesterday trying to get a present . . . Are you sure it's all right, Bobby?'

'Of course,' said Bobby. 'Don't be stupid. What did you get her?'

'Oh, we got her this amazing teapot. A nine-cupper. Oh, it's beautiful. She's forever complaining her teapot isn't big enough so that should sort her out.'

Bobby only half-listened as Suzanne told him all about the teapot and the joy they had in finding a nine-cupper. Suzanne was wearing new earrings and her make-up was bolder than usual. The way she'd look if she was going to a disco. The way she'd looked the first night he'd met her. A sense of jealousy, little more than a shiver, compounded with his dis-appointment and for a brief second Bobby succumbed to a feeling of desperation. He was well pissed off.

Suzanne got a few 'Hellos' as they walked past the queue for the pictures. She was very popular. Mostly people of her own age group but a few older ones Bobby didn't recognize.

When they got to the pub it was still quiet. Bobby was keen to get the drinks in and, as usual, drank his first pint very quickly while they chatted about work and college. Suzanne was looking nervous and self-conscious. She wasn't asking as many questions as she normally did, she was doing all the talking. Her make-up looked a bit clumsy in the light and made her look younger than Bobby liked. Bobby knew, though, that given the right photographer and the right conditions Suzanne could be made to look very beautiful.

Bobby got himself another pint. He thought about acting peeved, playing the spoilt brat, greet to get your way. But Suzanne was tough. He didn't know how she'd react. She could tell him to fuck off. Suzanne was looking at her watch and Bobby didn't know what to do.

'What you got planned for this week?' asked Bobby.

'A lot of studying,' said Suzanne, grinding her teeth. 'I'm well behind. I've got two lab reports and a three-thousand-word dissertation to be in by the end of the week. Then it's the exams.' She sighed. 'God, I need to do a lot of work.'

'You'll be all right. You'll pass.'

'That's what everybody keeps saying, Bobby. But what they forget is that I didn't do at all well in the mocks. I've really got to start working.' Suzanne looked at her watch again. 'Listen, I'll need to be going, all right.'

'So when will I see you next?'

'I don't know. I'm really going to be busy. I'll maybe pop round during the week.'

Bobby felt like he had the ticket but not the transport, the show would go on without him. He didn't want to push her – he knew he wasn't drunk enough to behave like that, anyway – but he wanted something. Not commitment, but a promise.

Bobby was distracted from his thoughts by a grip on his shoulder and the smell of fresh alcohol down his neck.

'Heh, Bobby, my man. How you doing there, eh?'

'Oh. Hello, George. You all right?'

'Yeah. I'm fine. Fine. Just tanning a few bevvies, like. Listen, what it is is, do you know a lassie called Sharon Allan?' Bobby shook his head but George continued. 'She works over at the hospital? No? It's just that I've, like, been out with her a few times and that but, well she's a bit weird, Bobby. I'm a bit wary of her.'

'No. No, I don't know her, George. Never heard of her.'

George turned to Suzanne. 'Excuse me. Do you – I'm sorry, dear, I don't know your name.'

'Suzanne.'

'Suzanne. Right. Nice to meet you, Suzanne. Do you – heh, are you at the nurses' home?'

'No, I'm at college.'

'Oh. You've never by any chance heard of a lassie called Sharon Allan, have you?'

'No. Sorry.'

'Sure?'

'Mmmmm hmmmm.'

'Oh.' George addressed himself to Bobby again. 'This lassie, Bobby, I'm telling you she is weird. I just want to find somebody that knows something about her. There must be somebody that knows her.'

'I'm afraid I can't help you, George.' Bobby was a bit angry.

'Well,' Suzanne was getting up. 'I'll need to be going. I'll try and pop round sometime but I'm going to be very busy. I can't promise anything. Very nice meeting you, George. I hope you find out about Sharon.'

'Is this you away, Suzanne?' said George. 'Listen, do you want a drink before you go?'

'No thank you, George. I must be off.'

'Right,' said Bobby, almost standing up. 'Hey, look, enjoy yourself. Have a good time. And try and pop round. Okay?'

'We'll see. Bye, anyway. Bye, George.'

Bobby and George watched her to the door and Bobby got a friendly wave and smile. Partly in sympathy for being left with George, he presumed.

'Heh,' said George. 'Nice bit of gear that. Bit snooty, though. You want another drink?'

Bobby stuck his hands in his pockets, crossed his legs at the ankles, let his head fall forward, sighed and said, 'Yeah. Why not?'

While George staggered up to the bar and attempted to get served, Drew Preston and his seven-strong pleasure-posse came tumbling in.

'Whoah-ho,' bellowed Drew upon seeing the recumbent

Bobby. 'Just seen your woman down the road there. She dumped you then?'

'Nah.' Bobby laughed. 'She's away out for a meal with her pals. What are you lot up to the night, anyway?'

'Eh, getting rubbered, I suppose,' said Drew.

'Then hitting some disco,' added Gus.

Bobby thought for a second, shrugged his shoulders and said, 'All right if I tag along?'

'The more the merrier,' said Drew. He furrowed his brow, looking as though he'd forgotten something, and added, 'And I intend getting paralytically merry.'

'Listen, boys.' George was back again. 'Do any of you know a Sharon Allan? A nurse? About twenty-two, twenty-three?'

'That lassie that stays up Clark-Maxwell Street?' said Gus. This was a reference to a girl who was suspected of being a prostitute and whose activities had taken on near-legendary proportions. Knowing glances sped round the table at George's expense. Laughter was held back in the hope of extending the ruse.

'You taking the piss?' said George.

Gus slapped his thighs as they all burst out laughing. 'See that,' he said. 'Quick as a flash. You can't fool George.'

'I just want to find out about this woman,' continued George with passion. 'She's a bit weird.'

'Are we talking whips here, George?' said Gus and now the laughter became uncontrollable with even Bobby joining in.

'Afraid we don't know her, George,' said Drew. 'Nobody knows her.' Drew furrowed his brow again and added, as though thinking aloud, 'Now that is weird.'

George left them. He wasn't going to find out anything here. 'I've got to find somebody that knows something about this woman. Got to.' He was mumbling to himself but anybody who'd wanted to could've heard him.

'He's a sad case, George, so he is,' said Drew.

'The guy's a fucking wanker,' said Bobby. 'There is no way he has ever earned the right to call anybody weird.'

'Did he scare off your ride?' asked Gus.

'Nah. She was going, anyway.'

'He's a poor guy,' continued Drew. 'It's that wee village, all that interbreeding. He's just not socially adjusted.'

'The guy is a serious fucking wanker,' asserted Bobby. 'It doesn't matter where he comes from. He's just a hanger-on, a loser. You know he comes up to me the night and goes "Oh, Bobby, my man. How you doing, sir?" like I know him or something. The guy's an embarrassment. He haunts me. Can he not understand that nobody likes him? Can he not just go away?'

'Who is this Sharon Allan, anyway?' said Gus.

'Fuck knows,' said Bobby. He started laughing and said, 'God help her, that's for sure.'

A couple of Drew's mates got a double round in and Drew decided it was time to tell his George stories again. Everybody had heard them before but they were soon in stitches as Drew regaled them with George on the 18-30 holiday package, George's mam and the carpet beater, George at Chris's party and George and the motorcycle gang. Bobby nearly wet himself at the last one.

Gus was keen to get going but once Drew got started it was difficult to interrupt him, let alone stop him. It was the back of eleven before they finally got round to talking about where they were going to be heading off to. One of the lads suggested going to Trax but Bobby said he didn't want to go there cause that's where Suzanne was going.

'How you and her getting on, anyway?' asked Drew.

Bobby raised his hand and wiggled his fingers. Iffy. He said, 'Don't know. Don't know what the score is with her at all.'

'You shagged her yet?' asked Gus.

Bobby shook his head.

'Dump her! For God's sake, dump her!' shouted Drew. 'What, does she think she's special or something?'

'Nah,' said Bobby. 'She's a nice wee lassie and that but . . . I don't know.'

Bobby and Gus continued the discussion on women while the rest of them were settling down to get pissed. Bobby didn't know Gus that well and was surprised at how sensitive the guy was. He told Bobby he'd go back with his wife tomorrow given half the chance but there was no way she would have him, so all he did now was party. He said he really missed the kid, though, and showed Bobby a picture of the youngster he called 'my son'. Bobby told Gus all the troubles he'd been having with Suzanne but how he really liked her, though.

'If she doesn't want to party,' said Gus, 'then leave her. Life's too short, Bobby. You just get into a lot of hassle when you start fucking bothering about things.'

Gus was a fast drinker and kept going up for rounds every few minutes. Bobby usually started fast then slowed down but he was keeping up with Gus as they discussed women and those they'd had in common. Bobby decided that Gus was a good lad and by the end of the bottle was telling him so.

A couple of the lads said they wanted to head over to the rave at Gibson's. But Drew, though, said that out of town casuals had been going there for the past couple of weeks and stirring up trouble. They were too drunk for dancing, anyway. The bell went for last orders and they decided they would go to The Warehouse. There was always trouble at The Warehouse but it was confined to individuals (female, generally) rather than gangs.

As they left, Bobby appropriated somebody's unfinished bottle of Newcastle Brown and drank it in the taxi as they drove over to The Warehouse. When he was finished with the bottle, Drew grabbed it from him and threw it out of the window.

Gus asked Bobby if he was feeling all right. Bobby said he was okay. He felt great. He'd decided he was finished with that Suzanne and he was just going to party.

'Good,' said Gus.

Gus and Drew were worried that the bouncers wouldn't let Bobby in when they saw the state of him. Bobby, though, had enough experience to affect sobriety when it was called for, and was amiable and polite as the bouncers looked him over and marked him with the invisible pen.

Outside it had been quiet with only taxis and a few stragglers going about. But inside, in what used to be the cellar of the pub upstairs, you couldn't move, you couldn't hear and you sweated like the meat in a kebab shop. While the males huddled round the bars and in corners, the females created the noise and the spectacle. They shouted and chanted and partied with jam on it. They weren't hippies or punks or four-sugars-in-the-coffee wee lassies. Some were old and all were old enough. You see them as shoppers on Saturday afternoons or when they pour into pubs on hen nights; factory girls or football supporters' girlfriends, if you like. Seriously out to enjoy themselves.

The disc-jockey played chart records and golden oldies. He got the women to sing along and play games. There were no pretensions.

Drew got the drinks in and him and his pals headed off to a corner. Gus went with them. Bobby just stood where he was and said he was going to survey the goods. Like a train-spotter or a birdwatcher, he didn't move about, he just got himself a good position and waited.

Despite the acres of naked flesh, most were non-starters. Bobby didn't like women, Bobby liked girls. Then he spotted her. Small. Very young looking. Black dress cut low at the front and back. She was blonde, though, and her hair was too short. So what? Her pal left her and she was on her own.

She's rubbing her chin against her shoulder again and again and again.

She's the aloof one. Chin rubbing shoulder. Quick, go for it.

'I used to have a dog that did that. Bing his name was. A collie. See when I'd be heading off to school, he'd be up there at the window every morning, waving us bye-bye. Great, he was.'

She's smiling. Well, say something.

'I like dogs. Ours died last year. Joey. A wee terrier.'

'*Joey*? Christ, that's a name for a budgie.'

'It's a nice name. I like it.'

'Suppose so. I still miss Bing. I mind one time . . .'

Yessss. It's so fuck-ing ea-sy. Like playing football with a kid. This is when I'm confident. I've astered the mart of bullshit and I'm pretty and I smile a lot. What more could they want? Oh, I've got that as well. There's at least five of them in here staring at me. Fucking great. I love it.

'. . . Fucking hate cats, though. Pointless little shits. Don't like cats *at all*. Can't handle them. Tell me, what have cats ever done for anybody? They're like fish – useless.'

'Oh, no. I like cats. They're clever and they keep themselves clean.'

Would you listen to that voice? Four, five, *six* sugars in the coffee.

'Cats, Christ. Come on: they don't smile, they're devious; they shit and piss everywhere . . . God, they all look the same.'

'Well, I like them – so there.'

I seriously liked the way you said that. You'll do. I knew you'd look better once I opened you up. I've given you Bobby's ring of confidence. I've made you feel special. They're all looking at you. You've attracted more attention in the last half-minute than you have all night. I love it. How old are you? Sixteen? Twenty? I'm twenty-six. Half-way to fifty-two.

'You want to dance?'

She's asking – wants to show me off – so I'm dancing.

'You're on. But I should warn you I'm a brilliant dancer.'

And I am. Wow, she's really trying. She can't take her eyes off me. She wouldn't dance this way with anyone else. Who's in the night, anyway? There's Linda the knockback queen. Don't know what she's got to tease about. She's not exactly what you'd call attractive. Ah, there's Catherine and her beautiful big bum. I wouldn't mind some of that. Do I smell hash? Yes, I do. That reminds me, that bastard John Stewart still owes me fifteen quid. *Bastard!* I've got a bit back at the flat. Wonder if she'll take a smoke. Of course she will. Won't you, my little darling. Come on, give us a cuddle. I can see my face in your forehead. Ha ha. *I can see my face in your forehead.* Oh, I want it. I don't want to waste tonight. You're thick, eh? Eh, you're thick? Look who's talking. We were made for each other. Just want to party. Down-to-earth party animal. Anything but a student. I bet you work at Scott's.

'Thank you. You are a good dancer.'

I even get a curtsy.

'That's nothing. You should see me unblock drains.'

What's she doing?

'You all right?'

'A-ha. I just need to go to the ladies.'

'What? On your own? Women never go to the toilet on their own.' God, I'm going over the top. 'Admit it, you're leaving me. Right, go on. See if I care.'

'Shut up, will you. I'll be back in a minute. You want me to get you another drink?'

'It's all right. I'll get them. What do you want?'

'A Taboo and Irn-bru.'

'*A what?*'

'Taboo and Irn-bru. That's what everyone's drinking. It's really good. You should try it.'

'Eh, some other time.'

'Right. I'll just be a minute.'

That's that. God, this place is going well downhill. Is he still seeing that dog? *Why does that guy always go out with dogs?* God, I'm pissed.

'Eh, a pint of lager and a Taboo and Irn-bru, please.'

Uh-oh. There's Margaret on the warpath again. It's all right, she's leaving. Where's my fags? Only two left. She'll have fags. They always smoke.

'Hey, slut-fucker. How you doing?'

'Drew, my man. Hey, I'm going to score, man. *I'm going to score.* What you been up to?'

'Getting pissed. There's a drink over there for you, sir.'

'Christ, I've just got another round in. See's it here anyway.'

'Who's the dame?'

'Dunno.'

'You're getting desperate, pal. You'll have people talking about you.'

'Fuck them. I know enough stories about them to piss myself laughing for the rest of my life.'

'Yeah, fuck them. The lot of them, just fuck them. Let's get pissed.'

'I am pissed.'

'Let's get, eh, more pisseder.'

'Ha ha. My pal Drew. Come here, man. I love you.'

'It's yours, pal. Go for it. Wake up with the pubic hairs at the back of your throat and the deodorant on your tongue. It's the only fucking way.'

'It is, eh? It is. I've got overtime the morrow, though. Up at eight, fuck.'

'Tell you what to do, right? See when you get up, you feel like shite, right? Well, here's what to do. Here's what to do. Just go to the bog, and look at yourself in the mirror and say, "At least I ain't George". Ha Ha.'

'You're a sick man, Drew. But that guy's a fucking wanker, eh? A serious fucking wanker.'

'Yeah. You going to see that lassie? Whatshername Suzanne?'

'Don't know, Drew. Don't know. She's just playing games, man. She's young, you know. She's a bit innocent.'

'Yeah. There's plenty of fish in the sea. You seen that new lassie in accounts?'

'SEEN HER? MAN, I'M IN LOVE WITH HER. She is something else. I think I'm in there. No. No, seriously. Honest. She's been giving me a good bit of the eye and that. Yeah, I'm well into her. Wee Ronnie's new woman, as well. I'd shag her. You know what he's like. Can't keep a woman for more than two weeks without going back to that Sandra.'

'I hear she's got kids, though.'

'Has she? Don't know about that then. Dodgy.'

'Here's your dame coming back. I better go. Hey, listen, I wonder if that's Sharon Allan.'

'Oh, Christ, man. Don't say that!'

'Ha ha. I'm telling you, sir. Your quality control's up the spout. Me, I've never fucked an ugly woman in my life.'

'I have. Nah, she's not that bad. Best looking lassie in here. At least I'm getting laid the night. Yessss.'

'Yeah, suppose so. See you, dude.'

'See you, man.'

Here she comes. She's all right. She's got a nice wee body. What does Drew know? He's never been laid in five years. They're all talk, that lot. Especially that Gus. That guy's disturbed. 'This is my son.' Jesus. Now look don't hassle me. Just party. Don't say 'Why . . . Why . . . Why'. Don't talk about horoscopes. Don't tell me all your problems. Talk about grannie this and grandpa that. No don't. Don't talk. Don't tell me about the guy that raped you. Just party. Okay?

'Hi. Who was that?'

'Dunno. Never seen him before. He just came over and started bugging me.'

'Sure.'

'Nah, that's Drew. He's an arsehole.'

'He looks it.'

Right, here goes.

'Look, I don't want this to seem like a come-on or anything, but do you fancy coming back for a coffee?'

It's like Christmas . . . a last-minute penalty . . . Have I got enough sugar? . . . Beddie bye-byes.

'Okay.'

Yessss.

'I'm a good judge of character. I can tell you're a nice person. I'll just get my coat. Be back in a minute.'

WHAT? *What you talking about?* What are you talking about? A nice person? I'm a bastard, for fuck's sake. It's a game, don't you realize that? And don't get possessive. I'm too pissed to do anything. Stop staring at me. Oh, God, here comes her pal. Why do they always look like that? Like her out of *Hi-De-Hi*. Whatshername? What's that dozy cow's name? That's what she fucking looks like, anyway. What's she wanting?

'Hey you. You can just fuck off. You hear me? Just fuck off. She just had a kid three weeks ago.'

Huh . . .

'So what? So fucking what?'

The Sue Pollard-lookalike pushed Bobby and Bobby pushed back. Before Drew and Gus could get to him, the bouncers had Bobby halfway up the stairs.

Bobby remembers nothing about this night and has a good laugh when people tell him about it. It's become one of Drew's 'Bobby' stories.

Suzanne never did come round. Bobby's bumped into her a couple of times and she's doing all right. Bobby himself has been out with three or four girls since.

Tonight he's up at the bus station, standing outside John Menzies – waiting for a girl who's fifteen minutes late.

The Finger In

Last Saturday down the town I bumped into Wee Rollo. We went to the Wimpey and sat beside Fiona Jones and Paula Sims. They were talking about their holidays. Paula kept staring at me and I stared back. She went to the same primary school as me. That's when I had a big rip in my pocket and I used to get all the girls to stick their hands in. I never wore pants. I suppose Paula did that. I don't remember. I loved it. I love showing off. When the teacher went out the room I used to leap on the table then drop my trousers and wave my bare arse at the door.

I'm going to get expelled again. I wrote on the blackboard a message for my woodwork teacher saying how proud I would be to kill that sorry little bastard. He picks on me. He says five-ten-bugsproof when I walk through the door. Everybody laughs at me. I think a lot about fighting him and throwing things at him. He makes a fool of me. He never passes my work. I got expelled the last time when I held a Black-and-Decker to Tracey Dodds' head and screamed like blazes. It wasn't plugged in. My mum made them take me back.

My mum was crying last night. I heard her up at the toilet. I heard her peeing. Me and my wee sister heard her peeing. I asked what was wrong but they wouldn't tell me. My mum's boyfriend was shaking and shouting but he never touched me. He calls me Bamber cause I look like Bamber Gasgoigne. I hate that bastard as well.

I think I'll steal Jamie's pen. He's all right. He'll say nothing. I wish he was my friend. He's hopeless at sports and woodwork too. But he tries in class and Mrs Munro likes him. I fancy Mrs Munro. I want to feel her tits and rub her bum. I want her to put her hand in my pocket. The other night I ripped my pocket cause I was thinking about that. When she's talking to the class that's all I'm thinking about.

The teachers don't bother about me. They like the ones that play in the school teams and the good-looking ones. *The snotties*. I got reported last week when I hit Stewart Miller over the head with a chair. It was perfect. His glasses fell off. It's like throwing a ball of paper into a metal bucket. Or jumping over a fence when nobody sees you. I like the control. I like the freedom. I like the skill. Everybody was looking at me. Nobody was laughing. They didn't understand I just wanted to knock his glasses off. It was funny.

It used to be that I got everybody laughing. Now hardly anybody laughs. They laugh among themselves at boring things. Like when they go on about parties, they go on about things that were boring as if they were really exciting. They don't do *anything*.

I'm starting to forget a lot of the things I do. It's other people that bring them up. They keep hassling me. It's as if they've got nothing better to do than remember things.

Hillsborough

John Peel has just played a record of Aretha Franklin singing 'You'll Never Walk Alone'. He tries to say something about the events at Hillsborough two days previous but breaks down.

This is the time of night I'm usually asked to do some babysitting or I'll get my visitors. If not then I'll be reading or watching the telly, I'll always try and have the radio on, regardless. It would be true to say I hear my favourites – and the ones that are going to become my favourites – but if it wasn't for the bits in between the records, I don't think I'd be listening.

These opinions and anecdotes and the general enthusiasm have played as much part in forming my character as anyone or anything has done. There's John's enthusiasm for his records and his family, his stories that shatter myths, debunking the past in favour of the present (and the future), and there's his love of football – in particular Liverpool Football Club. John's told me often about Billy Liddell's comeback and the time he embraced Bill Shankly after the European Cup Final. I remember Kenny Dalglish phoning him on his birthday one year. Kenny, though, preferred that the conversation wasn't broadcast. That didn't matter, it was okay. Like the best of my friends, John's just a fan.

As usual, I was at the Falkirk game on Saturday. Clyde were the visitors. I was with two friends I only ever see at the football. We met up in the pub beforehand and quickly exchanged news before moving on to the serious business of the day: discussing the craze for inflatables. We decided that Falkirk's would be the best: the inflatable bairn.

As we approached the ground we could hear the crowd giving great waves of cheers. This was a bit unusual. Either

we'd signed Maradona or the telly was there . . . The telly was
there and the camera was panning over the Falkirk end with
everyone hoping to figure in the opening shots of the coverage.

We talked about the game in prospect, praising our talented
youngsters and expressing disappointment with our prima
donnas who've been letting us down in our promotion chase.
'If only they could get a couple of seasons together . . . We need
to get rid of . . . The big clubs don't want us up . . . The town
doesn't want us up . . .'

I met and had a blether with an old friend from school. He's
the only person I see from school, and the only place I ever see
him is at the football. Him and his wee boy were both wearing
Falkirk tops. Every time I speak to him he goes on about how
we're the only two from our year who still go to all the games.
He's really disappointed by this, it's as if everybody else has
fallen by the wayside. I spotted a bloke from my new work
with two guys that could only be his brothers. It's been good
having somebody at my new work I could talk about Falkirk
with. We'd been looking forward to Saturday, looking
forward to being on the terraces and cheering on our team.
Keith, one of the friends I was with, told me that the old guy in
front of us looked a bit like my dad. And in a way he did. Kind
of respectable with a cool haircut. I get a sense of history when
I hear the old guys talking about sport. I mean, they went to
games when the crowds were absolutely massive. If you
believe them (and there's no reason not to) they were all at the
Real Madrid–Eintracht Frankfurt game. They can tell you all
about the Cassius Clay–Sonny Liston fights and how Roger
Bannister broke the four-minute mile. They've seen the Lisbon
Lions, the Famous Five and Jim Baxter. They've even seen
Falkirk winning the Scottish Cup.

Saturday was a beautiful sunny day. Falkirk won and scored
a couple of cracking goals in the process. Before, during and
after, the talk is almost always exclusively about football.
Anticipation in the pub, comment during the game and
analysis back at the pub. On Saturday, however, Keith
brought a radio to keep up with the Dunfermline score. He
relayed the news from Hillsborough: ambulance, abandon-

ment, death. There was little comment or analysis. Just a bit of confusion, a bit of sorrow. Just emptiness, really. In the pub afterwards the pictures appear on the screen. You make all the right gestures but you're never shocked and that hurts.

In the forty-eight hours since, I've watched all the news coverage and every current affairs programme. I was supposed to go out on Saturday night but I didn't. I stayed in and switched channels. Waiting for something. Some people talked sense. One guy compared the recent spate of British disasters with those more commonly found in the Third World when he talked about bad organization, poor facilities and overcrowding. Jimmy Hill said that for too long football had been content to contain rather than eradicate hooliganism. What both these men are saying is that people didn't care enough.

I've scored out tons of stuff I've written here. Most of it was hate-filled and directed at anyone I could think of. Nothing ever gets done about football cause nobody ever agrees. My friends and I can watch the exact same game from the exact same position and come away with completely different inter-pretations. It's a big part of the fun but it's also a big part of the problem cause it extends to how the game should be run.

I could talk football for hours on end. When I phone up friends in London we spend most of our time talking about football. When I go round to my dad we talk about football. When I meet new people I usually end up judging them by how much they know about football.

I could go on. But not just now. Cause just now I'm watching the goals from the Falkirk game. The commentator says, 'Alec Rae. Oh, goal of the season' and the camera cuts to a jubilant section of the crowd. When I freeze-frame I can see my pal from school, the lad from work, the bloke that looks like my dad, and me and my two friends. There's a lot of faces there I recognize.

John Peel finishes his programme by saying that he never believed he was capable of experiencing such grief over the deaths of people he'd never known.

Life on a Scottish Council Estate
Vol. I Chap. 2

So the blessed council rehoused me, and now I'm sandwiched between a couple who watch videos of *The Hit Man and Her* and a right weird-looking guy who spends all his time at the bookie's and owns only one record – Dire Straits 'The Walk of Life'. Thankfully, we managed to save my records and The Big Man kitted me out with a new suite and a top-notch TV, hi-fi and video. It was the least he could do. My family and friends have been very good to me. They're great, as Big Tony the Tiger says. Edwyn and English Edgar arrive. Bad news. They have chapped the doors of the thirty-three places in our wee town that you can buy dope and have come up with nothing. Big fat zero. Stuart comes round. He empties my buckets, hoovers my carpets and ransacks my furniture but there are no roaches to be found. I am keeping my new flat very tidy. The Tank brings round one of his videos to entertain us. It features a black woman constantly screaming, 'Shit on my chest! Shit on my chest!' The plot develops to incorporate a series of guys – who look like my dad's neighbours, incidentally – and they, you guessed it, shit on her chest. Wee Harry appears. (At the door, like, not in the film.) He says we are depraved. The Tank says it's all right but it's not as good as *Anal Inferno*. The Tank is a window cleaner in real life. Wee Harry says he knows where we can get a bit of dope but first we have to listen to something that is very important to him. This we agree to do. Wee Harry goes over to the hi-fi, removes a tape from his pocket and puts it in the machine. It is Mahler's Ninth Symphony. It is sad and depressing with the good bits few and far between. It is the story of Wee Harry's life . . . Wee Harry and English Edgar depart to get the dope. *Chap! Chap!* The new kids (Winston, Lee, Emma and Nicola) and a dog called Bongo (that's right, the same darn dog!) are at the door. Bad

news, they say. My psychotic big brother has found out my
new address. *Oh, no.* They tell me he got it off Hamish when
Hamish was trying to sell him a camera. I thank the kids for
letting me know and they remind me I'm babysitting on Friday
night. I tell them it would be best to check again tomorrow.
My visitors express their sympathies when I tell them the news.
Wee Harry and English Edgar return with Grant, a half a ton
of Bombay mix and a bit of dope. But there is to be no party. I
tell my visitors I have to face this alone and ask them to leave.
This they do . . . I am alone. I am absolutely pissing myself and
absolutely shitting myself. I hear 'The Walk of Life' coming up
from below and find myself singing along. I'm just a bit dis-
illusioned. The door goes. It's Carmel. She is looking for my
pal Mikey. I tell her my pal Mikey is back in London and isn't
due a visit for another couple of months. She is disappointed
and horny. She puts on my specially compiled Prince tape and
starts coming on really strong. I tell her about my psychotic big
brother finding out my new address. (I also suspect that fear
has made me impotent, but I do not tell her this.) Needless to
say, she departs pronto. I make myself a coffee and think about
things . . . I'm thinking . . . I would really like a fish supper. A
fish supper with two pickled onions. A fish supper with two
pickled onions and a Mars bar. There are five fish supper
establishments within five minutes walk of my house but I stay
glued to my settee. I hear the ice-cream van but still I do not
move . . . *I recognize that knock – it's The Big Man!!* He heard
about my psychotic big brother finding out my new address
and he's come straight back from the Middle East. He hands
me a sports bag and says it's the best he could do. I open the
bag. It's a fucking machine-gun! The Big Man explains the
mechanisms, praises the specifications and lists the various
conflicts in which it has been put to use. 'Just kill the fucker,'
he says. The Big Man's heart is in the right place. Respectfully,
I ask him to leave. He does so. I get back to my settee and look
at the machine-gun. Self-defence? An accident? I could hit him
with it. Oh, I could hit him with a lot of things. Somebody
chaps my verandah door. I think really fast. fkjfidkfjdkrick58
djrifjjdj jfjgjjkkrj. The Big Man must have locked the close

door. Now I live three flights up. Only one person would have
the audacity to climb that. *My psychotic big brother.* The door
gets chapped again. If I blasted off a few rounds that would be
the end of it. But my mum wouldn't speak to me if I killed my
psychotic big brother. And God knows what she'd do to me
for ruining the curtains. 'What do you want?' I enquire. 'It's
me, Hamish,' says Hamish. Whhhh-ooooh. I let him in. I tell
him about all the trouble he's caused. He laughs and says it
was all part of his masterplan. I point the machine-gun
between his legs and say, 'What masterplan was that, like?'
Hamish goes on to explain what happened. My psychotic big
brother saw Hamish trying to sell the camera and approached
Hamish with the intention of buying said camera. Once they
were alone my psychotic big brother inflicted various forms of
torture upon poor Hamish in order to find out my new
address. (I expect these acts of torture were never required to
go beyond threats, but, anyway.) So Hamish gave him my
address. (I expect these acts of torture were never required
to go beyond threats, but, anyway.) So Hamish gave him
my address and my psychotic big brother appropriated the
did was to phone the police and tell them he'd seen a guy with
a stolen camera. But the camera wasn't stolen I point out. Eh,
says Hamish, it was . . . cause he stole it from his work. It was
in the papers. So, continues Hamish, the police caught up with
my psychotic big brother as he was preparing to come round
and see me, i.e. getting tanked up on Newcastle Brown and
whisky. There ensued a struggle and my psychotic big brother,
five policemen, two Alsatians and three civilians have ended
up in hospital. My psychotic big brother will be facing several
charges and will almost certainly spend a while in prison,
Hamish, who knows about such things, assures me. I have
been reprieved. I go out onto the verandah and holler 'YEE-
HAA. BEEZER CITY, MAN.' Hamish asks me what I intend
doing with the machine-gun. He says he could sell it to
somebody over the old town and offers to go halfers. I shake
my head. Hamish is married with two children in real life. My
visitors return. There is much celebration. The Big Man has
bought me a fish supper with *three* pickled onions and a Mars

bar. We party well into the night. Grant pesters Wee Harry about his sister. The Big Man and The Tank have a kid-on fight. Hamish and Stuart have a real fight when they accuse each other of hogging. Edwyn and English Edgar party through in my spare bedroom. I play my records at ridiculous volumes and we finish off by having a game of indoor football . . . Within the week I am evicted for making too much noise.

A New Mirror

You look like shit.

Oh, thanks. That's just what I need.

How? What's up?

I don't know. Just pissed off.

What about?

I DON'T KNOW, RIGHT, *God, almighty* . . .

Okay. Okay. I just thought I'd come round for a blether and that. I haven't seen you for a while.

Well – I've no news and I'm looking like shit. Anything else?

Sorry.

Yeah, sure.

I am.

I'm just bored, right. Bored with this town, this life . . . Sometimes I don't even know why I bother living.

Don't say that.

Why for ever not?

. . .

. . .

Do you fancy going out?

Nnnnnoooo, I do not fancy going out . . . Why do you come round here?

You need to do something.

Oh, so you come round here and say 'You look like shit'.

Well, you do. You look grim. Is that better?

. . .

. . .

No, I don't fancy going out.

Okay by me. Want a fag?

Cheers.

Seen Eddie earlier. Had the new kid with him. Smart wee thing.

Yeah, I was there on Sunday, the afternoon. It's got her eyes

. . . There's a programme on about ospreys I want to watch. Do you mind if I turn the telly on?

Of course not. Don't be silly. It's your home.

. . .

. . .

. . .

It was good that. I never usually watch nature programmes.

I watch them all the time. They're fascinating.

I'll need to go now. I've got an early class tomorrow.

Yeah, well, thanks for coming round. I'll see you to the door.

Right.

Pop round again some time.

Sure . . . I promise not to say 'You look like shit'.

It's okay, don't bother about it.

Cheerio, then.

See you later.

See you.

The Girlfriend

And Susan'll always be the girlfriend. What X does Susan does. What Y does Susan does. Susan'll be the one to change. 'You don't have problems,' he says. So what are you then? Scotch mist? 'I've never even looked at another girl.' The last person said that was lying.

It's so transparent. Susan knows what's going on, all right. But Susan has feelings for the guy; not the hunk they think I dote on; not what they go on about; not the pleb he pretends to be – but what's hers. 'I've never even looked at another girl.' Yeah, and Susan died in the Vietnam War, pal.

Profound Experiences, Work and Friends

This hippy told me I should go away for ten years and have a profound experience then come back and write about it. I asked what he meant. He laughed and said I would know when it happened, and that I would go on to produce work of 'depth' and 'vision'. Ooooo-voooo. Patronizing git.

There's graffiti up the road proclaiming white power and it uses the word 'spirit'. *Spirit?* That sounds like it comes from the same dictionary as 'profound experience'. I'm not linking the individuals, just pointing out the vagueness and arrogance which I find disturbing. Most of the hippies I know are all right. They lack assertion and lucidity but are friendly enough.

Auberon Waugh wrote to me and said I was brilliant but that I should write more about work. Well, Auberon, it so happens I was working with a guy from Liverpool the other week (it wasn't Liverpool itself but one of those places you always assume to be part of Liverpool but actually isn't) and the guy told me about this estate down there where every dog was a fighting dog. He told me about badger-baiting as well: that's when a badger has its legs bound together with wire and is attacked by successive dogs. He's a really nice bloke and a gamekeeper so there was no reason for me to doubt what he was saying. I can tell you this stuff shocked me.

I went round to my dad's to phone up Auberon and tell him the news. My dad wouldn't let me phone London, though, so I had to content myself with a phone call to the hippy. I asked him if this was a profound experience. His reply was lost among his mumbling. I told him to get assertive. (That does the trick. See when I go to the football and shout 'Come on, lads. Get assertive' it really works!) The hippy got assertive and said that this wasn't a profound experience. It wasn't personal enough. Darn it, as Rock Hudson used to curse.

Now I'm the sort of person friends come up to and say 'I

haven't told anybody this, and I don't know why I'm telling you, but . . .' I get it all the time. (I'm terrified of talking to strangers at bus-stops cause I know they're going to start telling me their life stories.) I worked out one night that there are forty-seven people in the world who have good reason to hate my guts – but only thirty-one of them know about it. See, I juggle a lot of lies in my life. A lot of these things I'm told are very nasty, very unpleasant and very personal . . . Then I sit here and try and make something of this wee world. Some things, though, remain unwritten. But they're always there, at the back of my thoughts. I'm left with the truth and nothing but the truth (apart from the bit about Auberon writing to me) – but not the whole truth. I try my best. I went round to my dad's and phoned up the hippy and told him my dilemma. He told me not to bother cause all that stuff had been written before. He told me I'd be better off writing science-fiction, fantasy, magic-realism, poetry, fables, historical things etc. He was fair chuffed with his response. He's really into science-fiction and gave me lots of encouragement. I'm not so sure. I told him how my dad never let me watch *Doctor Who* when I was a wee boy cause he said that if I watched that kind of stuff I would grow up to be an intensely boring bastard and nobody would like me. The hippy hung up.

Anyway, that was a really short short story about profound experience, work and friends with references to racist graffiti, badger-baiting and the problems of pretending to be a writer in real life.

I Told Her That I Loved Her and That

I don't need to be nice about these things.

'Hello, everybody. How you doing? Listen, we're running a bit late the night so, eh, we better get a move on; you know what the curfew's like in this town. Okay, eh, this one's called "Sweet Thursday". It's about getting your giro and going out and getting pissed. Yeah. One-two-one-two-three-four . . .'

The guy on the keyboards, I know you, don't I? Hugh Johnson's your name. Yeah, you were the one who always wanted to be my best friend at school . . . And I know you, dear. Didn't you used to hang around with Linda and her team? That's right. Can't remember your name, though. Yes, I am watching you, supplying your oo-oo's, singing and dancing. You're quite pretty. I don't have any guilt about this. I've paid one-fifty, you're performing and – ha ha – I get to study you. I can't be bothered with all this non-sexist rubbish. I wonder who she's shagging? The frontman?

She's looking over at those two guys I heard talking about her earlier. They were on about your sister. One of them said she 'wasn't very good' and that she 'had a cunt like the Mersey Tunnel'. Really nice thing to say that. They're drunk, of course.

I can't get drunk these days. I drink and drink but I don't get drunk. Sometimes I won't remember what happened but I won't feel drunk. Drunk as in silly and happy.

'Thank you. Thanks very much. You're, you're more than kind. Right, this one's for Ben and Helen. We'd like to thank them for helping us find a place to rehearse . . . Eh, thanks to Ben and Helen. Right, this is called "Mismanagement". It's about bureaucracy. I tell you, my life seems to be one long hassle with red tape . . .'

And mine's, pal; mine's is one long hassle over someone who said it would be best if we never seen each other again – give me red tape anyday.

You'd never guess I'd been stung. I can't get drunk yet I'm always drinking; I can't sleep yet I'm always tired; I'm never hungry yet I never eat.

Oh, she meant it all right. She wasn't angry – that's not her style – she was *pragmatic*. There was me pouring my heart out and for all the good it did I'd have been as well playing a blank tape.

Anyway, that's that and this is this. This is the after-taste – being on your own: making every meal, doing all the washing, paying every bill and buying every message . . . or not as the case is. I don't like it one little bit and I'm making a right mess of it. The flat's a tip. I'm fed up getting myself out of bed in the morning. I lie there and I sweat and stink and I don't want to go out. These smells that used to be wonderful are now disgusting. At nights I worry something's going to happen to me. I should see a doctor. I've got symptoms. People go to doctors all the time. The women at my work go every other bloody day. But I haven't been to the doctor's since I was a wee boy. I'm frightened he'd advise me to see a psychiatrist. That's what happened to Robert. These comparisons keep coming up. Women live longer than men, don't they? Huh, typical male, thinks a woman at the doctor is looking after herself, doesn't realize she's ill. I'm getting like my friends. Blaming women when it all breaks down. I'll be going back to them, I suppose.

'Oops. Sorry about my lead coming out there. We hope it didn't spoil your enjoyment too much. See that bastard Doogie never turned up the night. I can tell you right here and now, he's getting well dug up for that – he was supposed to be bringing the drugs. Anyway, we're hoping to bring this one out as a single when we, eh, when we get the money thegether. All donations welcome, incidentally. It's about what happens when your friends let you down. It's called "Fuck Off and Die". No. No, that's just my little joke. It's actually called "How Much It Meant To Me".'

Yeah, I'll be going back to the old team. I'll be going back to them because our entire social life revolved around her. She was the popular one, the one who wanted to get on. Our friends were her friends to begin with. I lose all of that. It's

unimportant, I know, but it adds to that after-taste. I feel
they're all against me. It's like I've fallen out with everyone. I'll
use these things to make me more upset. I know I will.

I should get the phone in. Just in case something does
happen to me. What happens when your appendix bursts and
you're on your own and you don't have the phone? I'll write to
her to tell her I have the phone in. I'll give her my number. I
know she'd use it. I'd be drunk and she'd phone me. She'd
express concern about me. She'd ask about my work and my
sister. As long as I answered her questions it would be all right.
If I started giving it my usual pish, she'd hang up.

I get so confident when I'm talking about me. I'm so full of
myself I'm boring. If you think about things all the time you'd
imagine that when you opened your mouth it would all make
sense to other people. Not true. Cause there's this understanding you get when you're low that gives you power
almost, it's manic and that's not nice. Diminished responsibility, they call it. Like rapists and child-molesters get
explained away by equating their backgrounds with their
actions. You know I really feel like using somebody. I could
phone Susie or Rachel, play on old affections.

'Right thanks. Thank you. This next one's for Sid and
Shona. Congratulations on the engagement, guys. This is a
love song. Ahhhh. It's about having to say you're sorry. This is
called "Roses and You" . . .'

Sorry means you never got away with it. Sorry means till
death do we bullshit. Sorry means: look, piss off.

The last words she ever said to me were, 'There's things you
don't know'. It sounds like the beginning of a conversation but
she wasn't talking about gossip, she was talking about me.
Treating me like I was a kid again. I'm not old enough, or
smart enough, or understanding enough; I'm not a woman,
not her. I don't know. Maybe it *was* just a reference to gossip,
secrets.

The last words I said to her were beauties: 'I think about you
more than he does.' I'd have been as well to put a gun to my
head right there and then. It sounded like the most important
thing in the world for me to say. *Correction*. It sounded like

the *smartest* thing in the world. Possessive and arrogant. I tried to be more than honest. But I was left with bullshit on my face – cause that's what it was. She won. At any rate, I assume her to be happy. That can't always be true, of course.

I could go and see her. She owes me money and she's got records of mine. *Huh,* that would be so typical of me. *Hi, how you doing? By the way, you owe me money, you've got records of mine and can we get back together again, please.* All I want to do is make a lot of sense. She'd say: *here's your money, here's your records and by the way, I think you're laughable.*

'Thanks again. Thank you. Right, this is a new song . . . yes, Rab, you heard me right; a – new – song. We just finished it there on Tuesday. We like it and we hope you like it, too. So, ladies and gentlemen – and Rab – this is the state of our art, and it's called "Whose Dream?". It's about how they fob you off with ETs and YTSs instead of creating real jobs with real wages. RIGHT! . . .'

Shut up, shut up. Why do people suddenly become ugly when they start going on about politics? This country's full of them. The ugliest, boriest bastards in the world.

I'm getting angry again. Something made me angry. I've got to do something. I want to show how much I hurt. I feel like smashing that guitar and that drumkit. Those two guys next to me are getting on my tits. They keep swaying and bumping into me. They're horrible: horrible clothes, horrible hair, horrible faces.

Calm down, calm down. Look, go to the toilet. Get another drink. Get something to eat. Shift your position. Just go to the toilet. Rinse your wrists. *That works.* Okay? . . . Okay. I better go and see somebody tomorrow. I'll give my folks a call. No, I'll go and see them.

. . .

That's better. She's staring at me again. Probably half the guys in here think that. Hey, I'm normal!

'That was the new song and, eh, it was a fucking disaster. We'll need to put some more work into it. Sorry about that. This, you'll be pleased to hear, is not a new song. It's an old song. It's our version of the Scritti Politti number, "Lovesick".

I like this cause it's weird. You can get away with things in a pop song. You can get away with being a bastard . . .'

You can? Yeah, you can.

Lots of oo-oos for her this time. She's still got her eye on me. They're not bad, really. The frontman's got charisma and the musicians are competent. They're enjoying themselves and giving pleasure to others. Stretch that to a hundred words and that'll do. Stick their photo in again. Their mums'll like that.

I should do something, do something positive. I'm spending too much time depressed and too much time thinking about it. Too much time thinking about writing and phoning and going to see somebody that just isn't interested. It's absolutely finished.

Oh, I told her that I loved her and that. Told her often, in fact, but it's only now I'm beginning to realize what it meant. Like last Thursday evening when I was curled up nice and cosy on the settee. The sun was blazing in and I was waking up and going to sleep all the time. I just felt so good. I wasn't going through memories or dreaming of reconciliation, it was just a warm tingly feeling reminding me that I had been, and that a part of me still was hopelessly besotted. You can't take that away.

Hopelessly besotted with someone who looks like Michelle from *Eastenders*; who wears a frosted denim jacket and a white mini-skirt; whose hair is too thick and too short; who walks like she's wearing flippers; whose tits are too big and who's got a voice like chalk on blackboard; Jesus, this is what all the fuss is about.

'Right, thanks. Thanks a bundle. You've been a really great audience, as they say. This is our last number. We'll be back here on the twenty-third, be sure and tell your friends. We hope to see you then. Thanks for coming along. This last song's called "Got To Be Me". It's about a lassie I used to know who was murdered over the docks. I don't know, some of you might remember it. It didn't get a lot of coverage. Anyway, this is how I felt about her, thanks.'

I remember that. She was really nice. That was at school. This guy's singing a happy love song about a girl that was murdered.

My shoulders are drooping and my gut's starting to ache. That emptiness is taking over. I think I'll get in touch with Joe, see if he's going to the game on Saturday. I'll go out and buy some clothes as well. Leave myself less money to spend on drink. Maybe even make an appointment with the doctor. That's how you live with things.

God, they've turned the lights on. *My eyes.* Last orders. I've had enough. Maybe get some pakora for walking down the road. Get the sauce all over my clothes, as usual. What's the point of being a prat if you can't look like one?

She's looking at me again. She's pleased with herself. They've done well. No, I won't raise-my-hands-in-the-air-and-wave-them-about-like-I-just-don't-care - so there. My shirt'll come out.

'I've got no skin-like leather/no smart one-liners/no sure-fire schemes/nothing/but/daydreams/that it could be/me/oh, it's got to be me . . . Thank you. Thanks very much. We're *Horn for Diana* wishing you good*night*.'

Bizarre. They're finished and I'm off. She's coming over to talk to me. Wonder what she's going to say?

'Excuse me. You're the guy from the local rag, eh? Are you going to give us a good write-up?'

You never know, I don't need to be nice about these things. *Don't say that.*

'Well? What's the matter? Cat got your tongue?'

'Eh, no. I just, eh, well, eh . . .'

'Christ, you're pissed.'

'No. No. No. No, I'm not drunk. You don't understand. I can't get drunk. I can't get drunk.'

'Fuck off, pisshead!'

They Are Twenty-One Years Old

'What's that?' asked Mary.

'Lagging for the boiler,' said Roy as he piled the shiny orange material into the wash basket behind the door.

'Where'd you get it?'

'The work. Lifted it, like. Everybody does. It's fucking good stuff. Better than that rubbish your mother gave us. I'll put it on later.' Roy sat himself down at the table, took out his tin and made a needle-thin roll-up. 'Get the kettle on then,' he said. 'Did you cash that giro?'

Mary pointed to the money on top of the fridge. She bit her lower lip.

'IT'S SHORT.'

'I went to the van.'

'JESUS, WOMAN, HOW MANY TIMES DO I HAVE TO TELL YOU?'

'IT WAS RAINING!'

'STUPID BITCH. FUCK YOU!'

The grocer charged 5 per cent when you cashed your giro at his van. Mary knew this but didn't want to go over the town. She liked going to the van, anyway. She got to see the neighbours and didn't have to get changed.

Mary poured Roy a cup of tea and helped herself to a roll-up from his tin. She only smoked when he was in.

'Christine fell off the high chair the day,' said Mary.

'She okay?'

'I think so. I checked her eyes.'

'When's Robert seeing the speech therapist?'

'Eleven the morrow.'

'Right, mind you and go this time. That kid's weird. Wearing nappies at that age, for Christ's sake.'

Robert was three, Christine just six months. Both children were playing on the floor. The baby was too young to be anything but beautiful. Robert, though, was pale and hot and sickly looking. He still picked at things – plaster off the walls, paint off the radiators, wood off the fireplace – and stuck them in his mouth. Robert wasn't Roy's.

'Whose is the coffee?' asked Roy.

'Ours. Helen brought it round. She nicked it, like. Got cheese as well.'

'Your sister, Christ. What's she like?'

'She's good to us!'

'I know that. Just wish you could get a word in edgeways sometimes, that's all.'

'She was on about the dog.'

'I told you, it's just worms.'

The dog was through in the living-room. It was skin and bone. Exercise meant being let out the front of the close to do its business, or a visit over the road to Mary's mum. One of the neighbours had reported them recently on account of the dog. Complaining that it did the toilet on the stairs and was responsible for rummaging through the bin-bags. When the neighbour challenged Roy about this, Roy kicked the dog in the face and said, 'There, you happy now? It won't do it again.'

Roy went over to the sink and started peeling potatoes for chips. He made the chips because Mary had already caused two chip-pan fires this year.

'When'd you put the pies in?' asked Roy.

'Five.'

'Good.'

'Where you off to the night?'

'The Lion,' said Roy. He went out every pay-day. 'Meeting George and Bill at the cashline at half-nine. Telling you, them wages better be in the night. *What's she laughing at upstairs?* SHUT UP! FUCKING COW!' Roy grabbed the brush and banged it against the ceiling with three short, violent jabs. 'I'm going to the council about that bitch.'

'See Lynn's pregnant again,' said Mary.

'So,' said Roy.

'I'm just saying.' Mary paused before adding, 'It's not his.'

'Who's is it then?'

'I DON'T KNOW, ROY.'
'DON'T YOU FUCKING SHOUT AT ME!!!'
'DON'T YOU HIT ME . . . DON'T.'

'Fuck off. I'm warning you.' Roy let his words trail off and diverted his attention to the chips.

Mary's brothers had given Roy a doing the last time he hit her. A bad one. Mary had headed straight for her mother's after he had hit her. Mary's brothers (three of them) came round, dragged Roy out onto the landing and, for all to see, caved his head in, smashed his face up, and for good measure cracked a couple of his ribs.

Roy was wary and a little timid in the wake of that episode. Coupled with his gawky appearance this made him look less of a nutter and more of a misfit. He'd been charged a couple of times, for assault and breaking and entering. He'd narrowly missed a prison sentence for the latter. On the face of it he was no more frightening to look at than most but he worked out with weights and everything he did, he did aggressively. Although he knew a lot of people, he had few friends, his company just those he met in pubs. Roy had wanted to join the army but Mary wouldn't let him.

Mary hadn't been feeling well recently. She had difficulty in sleeping and told the doctor she had spells of double vision. The doctor carried out tests and had referred her to the hospital to get her ovaries checked out. Mary had virtually no social life, only her family and occasionally a few words with neighbours. The neighbours generally avoided her on account of wanting nothing to do with Roy. Mary had a limp which she had carried through from schooldays. This hadn't been a happy time for Mary. She wasn't very popular and had been nicknamed 'The Boke'.

The flat was spartan but tidy. Roy had made a good job of laying the carpets and fitting the linoleum. He'd papered the living-room and painted everything that needed to be painted. All this had taken him less than a week, and he'd been working during the days. The previous week they'd had a satellite dish installed. Mary was pleased. This meant Roy wouldn't be going out as much. So there would be less chance of him getting into trouble.

'Come on, black bastards.' Roy addressed the chips. 'Where's my tin?'

'Top of the fridge, where you left it.'

'See it.' Roy reached over for his tin and rolled himself another cigarette. 'The van been round yet?'

Mary stretched over the sink so that she could see out onto the court and said, 'It's there. What you wanting, like?'

'Get us fags, some Irn-bru and something for the kids.' Roy smoked real cigarettes when he went out. He handed Mary a fiver and said, 'Got a sub off Charlie just in case you hadn't cashed that giro. I'm telling you, the wages better be in the night.'

Mary took the crisp fiver and unfolded it. She didn't want Roy to go out. She knew there would be trouble. There always was. She didn't want him to get hurt. She still felt something for him. As Mary studied the fiver she said, 'What's happening with that jewellery?'

'Dave pawned it. Just leave it for a while. It's hot. It's worth eight hundred quid, Mary. That's a lot of money.'

'What you doing with the money you got?'

'Ha. That's blown. That was last Saturday.'

Mary turned to leave. Just as she was about to go she said, 'Pawned it? What address did he give?'

'CHRIST, WOMAN, WILL YOU STOP ASKING SO MANY QUESTIONS? WHAT ADDRESS DO YOU EXPECT HIM TO GIVE? STUPID BITCH! FOR CHRIST'S SAKE, HE GAVE HIS OWN ADDRESS . . . What are you laughing at. WHAT YOU FUCKING LAUGHING AT?'

Baby on a String

'Three hundred and forty-two, three hundred and forty-three . . .'

Ken laughed as he waited at the top of the stairs. 'So this is your excuse for not coming to see us, Jim,' he said. 'The stairs getting too much for you?'

'I'm decrepit,' said Jim. 'Was that barking I was hearing?'

'Yeah, the wee fellow. He goes his dinger even with the neighbours' buzzers.'

Jim struggled up the last few steps and said, 'From the sound of it I thought maybe you'd started smoking again.'

'Nah, not me.' Ken laughed. 'No way.'

They entered the flat. 'Christ, it's warm in here, sir,' said Jim and made a face to show he was suffering. As he unzipped his jacket a ball of white fur came bombing to greet him.

'Hiya, Booboo, my man! Was that you making that racket? Who taught you that then? Eh?' Jim pushed the puppy to one side then the other until it rolled over, then he tickled its tummy. 'He's getting big, eh?' added Jim.

'He is that,' said Ken. 'He's a fat, lazy shit. *Aren't you?*'

Jim lifted the dog as though it were a dumb-bell and followed Ken through.

Katrina was kneeling on the floor, looking through the cassettes. Wogan was on the telly but the sound was turned down. Katrina smiled when Jim came in and said, 'Hello, stranger. Did you hear the barking?'

'I was just saying to Ken there, it sounded like he'd started smoking again.' They all laughed. Jim looked around and added, 'Well, I must say, you've fair tarted this place up.'

'Shows how long it's been since you were last here,' said Katrina. 'Do you like it?'

'Yeah it's smashing.'

'We've spent a bit of money on it . . .' started Ken, looking at Katrina.

'But it's been worth it,' finished Katrina, looking at Ken.

Jim stood in the middle of the room. He didn't like it. Whereas previously it had been affably ramshackle, it now resembled nothing so much as a waiting-room in a BUPA advert: pale blue walls, straight-edged black furniture, popular prints and masses of over-sized plants. But it was too cramped, it needed a more spacious room. It was as though they'd followed a recipe without acknowledging the proportions. It hadn't been developed, it had been bought. If a room reflects personality then Ken and Katrina were telling the world they were boring bastards.

Theirs was one of the less troublesome closes in the scheme of flats. The verandah looked over to the better council houses – the four-in-a-block estate. This was where Katrina's parents stayed, and where Jim lived with his mum and older sister.

'Anything special you want to hear?' asked Katrina.

'I'm not fussy,' said Jim.

'I'll put on The Waterboys, you like them.'

'Brookie's on shortly,' said Ken. 'See if Paul Collins has his heart attack.'

'Hope so,' said Jim. 'I like that unit. Where'd you get it?'

Katrina was pleased and said, 'Myra at work. *You know?* Shuggie's sister. It's incredible, eh? I love the finish, it's almost black. We got it for next to nothing, as well, eh, Ken?'

'Yeah,' said Ken who didn't consider fifty quid next to nothing.

It was small and fitted nicely into the corner, noted Jim. Katrina, though, had gone and stuck a huge pot-plant on top of it. Like getting your hair done then wearing a hat.

They talked for a while about mutual friends and families. Jim delighted in supplying the gossip. He was sarcastic and quite funny as he told of who was getting married, who was getting dumped and who was having trouble. This was a role Jim took upon himself: going round and seeing everyone and telling them about each other. He'd known Katrina from way back. She used to be best pals with Jim's younger sister.

Katrina asked if there had been any news from her. While Jim went on to talk about his family Ken went through to the kitchen to make coffee.

Paul Collins didn't have his heart attack on *Brookside* and that horrible Rogers family took up most of the show with Jim supplying his spot-on impression of father and son, Frank and Geoff. Jim said that although he was out most nights he'd never missed an episode of Brookie since the programme started. He always got people to turn the telly to the channel he wanted when he was in their houses. He recalled all the great sporting events and where he'd seen them: the great snooker matches, tennis matches and athletics. He liked getting people involved in the tensions.

'We're having a party for Katrina's twenty-fifth,' said Ken. 'You're invited, of course. Just a few folk.'

'Thanks. Hope you don't want a present.'

'I most certainly bloody do. A good one. Mmmmm, let me think . . . velvet curtains. That'll do. And, hey, remember this isn't one of your mates' parties; you don't turn up with twelve cans of Dutch and drink everyone else's.'

Jim laughed and said, 'Not like the old days, eh? Your folks away on holiday and everybody trashing the place. Mind that time your sister threw up over the bathroom door?'

'How could I forget?' said Katrina. 'And muggins had to clean it up.'

'They were great times,' continued Jim. 'Out of our heads we were. You couldn't move for couples winching downstairs, then you got the lucky ones upstairs . . .'

'I never made it upstairs with a girl at a party,' said Ken interrupting.

'Really,' said Katrina, surprised.

'Yeah. Absolutely true, I'm afraid. Always wanted to, just never got to, that's all. It never happened. I was really paranoid about it when I was younger.' Ken paused and added in mock-sanctimonious tones, 'And just out of interest, with whom did you go upstairs, my beloved?'

'Mmmmm, I'd rather not remember. I was very drunk. I was very, very drunk.'

'It's all right,' said Ken. 'It's all part of growing up.'

Katrina shared his smile. She rubbed his knee and said, 'Never mind, I'll take you upstairs one day.'

Ken turned to Jim and whispered, 'Actually, the reason I never went upstairs with a girl at a party was because all the parties I ever went to were in flats.'

Katrina sighed then slapped him about the ear. She faked a huff, picked up the mugs and ambled through to the kitchen.

Jim was thinking about the incident to which Katrina had referred. It wasn't important. He'd often wondered what had happened to that guy, though. Jim thought about going back to his party stories but refrained. Ken didn't know half the people Jim went on about.

'Managed to get all that Artex off the kitchen,' Ken said. 'Murder, it was.'

'Should've gave us a shout.'

'Nah, you're all right. Just emulsioned it for the now. Maybe get some tiles for around the sink. See what the boss says.' He looked over his shoulder to the kitchen.

Jim laughed. 'You ever think of buying a place,' he said.

'Funny you should say that . . .' Ken looked to the kitchen again, and added in a voice loud enough for Katrina to hear. 'Well, *I* think we'd do better putting money by for a deposit.' Ken lowered his voice again. 'But this is her first home and she wants it a little palace, regardless of how long we're going to be here. It's understandable, I suppose.'

'JESUS CHRIST, WHAT WAS THAT?' Jim bolted from his seat and rushed over to the window. He was shaking. 'It was a baby,' Jim muttered.

Ken went out onto the verandah and looked down. 'It's okay,' he said. 'It's just those nutters upstairs. They've got a doll dangling from a bit of string. They're teasing Sally Anne down below . . . I think they've got it in for Catherine.'

Voices could be heard coming from the upstairs verandah. Shouting something then repeating it until it was understood. It was loud enough, it was just difficult to comprehend. Katrina came through and asked Jim what was up. He shrugged his shoulders, still worked up and annoyed with himself for being so alarmist.

Ken came back in and explained what was going on. 'They're fucking nutters them,' he said. 'They stay in all the time playing those soundtracks to *Grease* and *Dirty Dancing* all day long. That's all they do. You can tell when they're asleep cause there's no noise.'

'They get up at half-one,' added Katrina. 'They get up to watch *Neighbours*.'

As if on cue the soundtrack to *Dirty Dancing* came booming through the ceiling. Katrina shut the verandah door and put The Waterboys back on to deaden it.

'That's Chris and Sylvia, eh?' said Jim.

'That's them,' said Ken. 'They of the infamous bed parties.'

'I know,' said Jim. He laughed.

'I wish they would go for the record and have one that lasted a year,' said Katrina. The bed parties were when Chris and Sylvia remained in bed with only a crate of wine and chocolates to sustain them. They could keep this up from one signing-on day to the next.

'Weirdos,' said Ken.

'It takes all sorts,' said Jim, ever the champion of freaks and weirdos.

Katrina butted in. 'It's different when you live beside them, Jim. You don't know what it's like.'

Jim had been silently sarky to himself about Ken and Katrina and their lifestyle. Now they were turning on him. It was as if they knew what he was thinking. He said, 'You don't go out much either.'

'No money to go out, Jim,' said Ken.

'I know you think we're boring,' said Katrina.

'No, I don't.' Jim stopped. He didn't like this situation. Something was wrong. He thought to himself: if you stayed in bed you wouldn't have to bother about getting out on the wrong side. Katrina was watching him with that look of silent, polite anger – as if she really *did* know what he was thinking. As if it was that obvious. Jim gave a shrug to accept some blame, but he didn't know what was wrong.

'We need to go to our bed soon,' said Katrina. 'Ken's to be up early for work.'

'Yeah, I know,' said Jim, rising. 'And I don't work, do I?'

Ken looked on while all this was taking place. Katrina turned up the volume of the stereo and shook her head. Ken knew he wasn't a part of this, whatever it was. He wouldn't have objected to staying up for a while, blethering away. He said, 'Well, thanks for coming round to see us, Jim. We don't get many visitors.'

'Okay. Cheerio then. Cheerio Booboo.'

Katrina didn't get up to see Jim to the door. Normally Jim would keep them standing at the door for ages, talking away for half an hour or so. But Katrina was angry, sitting on her hands, like an MP abstaining.

As Jim walked down the hall he could hear her shouting, 'See you later, big man' above the noise of the stereo.

'Right, take care of yourself,' came Jim's reply.

As Jim made his way down the stairs, Ken told him not to leave it so long until his next visit. And Jim said he wouldn't.

Jim thought about the baby on a string. If that hadn't happened he wouldn't have got so worked up and confused. But something in him kept bubbling up. If he'd restrained himself it would have been denial, not the real him.

As he crossed the bridge to the four-in-a-block estate, Jim looked at his watch. It was still early; time enough for a couple of pints. He looked back to see their bedroom light going on and a shiver ran through him. Not the same shiver as the baby on a string, this wasn't shock and fear, this was anger and jealousy. Because where Katrina was concerned he suspected his whole life was denial.

There's no point in me asking 'What was all that about?' so I ask Katrina if she's all right, if Jim had upset her.

'It's okay,' she says. 'I'm just very tired, that's all.'

She's working herself to the bone up at the hospital, and it's starting to show.

Presently, we have two levels of conversation: the chatty one and the intense one. I'd like to talk about what happened, but being chatty would be stupid and being intense would be dangerous. I want to tell her I don't mind her friends coming round, the old boyfriends and Jim, that I like them even. It's something I try to avoid.

When Anne visited last summer Katrina was very possessive. I always try and be open about my past to avoid contradicting myself as much as anything, but I couldn't have anticipated what happened later that night. Katrina kept asking questions, stupid things like birthdays. *I mean what difference is a birthday?* It wasn't private stuff she wanted to know, just details, like she was filling in a form or something. Anne's right working class and she's loud and very funny. She's a bit like Jim in the way she goes on about old friends. She remembers folk I've forgotten and gives personality to people I barely ever knew. I can't help but be impressed and interested. Katrina's questioning upset me a bit that night. These things just weren't important.

'Do you think Jim'll come back soon?' I ask.

'Mmmmm-hmmmm. He's like that. He blows up and storms off. He'll be away to the pub now.'

I don't think he was the one doing the blowing up, Katrina. But I don't say that. I say, 'He's a bit of a waster.' I don't really mean that. I just want to dismiss him. The guy just does not like me. He's forever going on about 'ordinary folk' and 'salt of the earth punters' and how much he respects them. I'm the newcomer and the outsider. I wear a collar-and-tie to my middle-management job. I might as well be the antichrist. He's got a cutting tongue and can make me feel like shit cause I don't fit in and I don't belong. You can't tell him anything, he's heard it all. He wasn't there but somebody told him. Everything he says is challenging, correcting and superior. He's an arrogant cunt.

I'll never forget the look he gave me the first time I met him. We were all in the pub and I got introduced to him. Everything seemed all right and we blethered away. Then I went up to the bar and caught him staring at me. I smiled at him and that's when he gave me that look. The sort of look nutters give you from the back of the bus. He's never done it since. Once was enough. He just smirks these days. He does it all the time.

Katrina says, 'Do you think we should move?'

'I'd like to. Not far. Just different. I want out of this flat.'

'I don't want to leave the town,' she says. 'I'm not leaving my mum. It's like running away.'

'We're not running away. People run away when they're unhappy.'

'Are you happy?' asks Katrina with a big enough smile to let me know she is.

'Yes, I am.' I want to tell her I'm happy because she knows me better than anyone else does but . . . 'But there's bad bits. Bits I could do without. I could do without Maureen.' Katrina laughs. Maureen's my other ex. Whenever I'm asked to list my dependants, I feel I should mention her, she's that much of a burden. She's pregnant this time and really let herself go. She comes round here expecting me to tell her what to do. I should never have got involved with her in the first place. This is the woman who wrote off my car, my brand new car. God knows what she'll do next. I don't want her and her problems for the rest of my life.

Katrina is asleep now. I've never known anyone who could fall asleep so quickly. She's the first thing I'll see when I wake up in the morning, and I'm watching her now like I'll be watching her then. I'm watching her hair and her cheeks and her mouth, all asleep.

There was no pool table or space so there were no louts or neds. The taped music was well in the background: sub-James Last like the soundtrack to a porno film. A low profile pub.

She took her time pouring the pint – the way it should be done – topping it off by forming a shamrock with the last few drops. Pure genius. Jim remained at the bar and started talking to the guy next to him.

The guy's about forty but contrives to look fourteen. He's wearing a shirt, a jumper, a jacket, trousers and shoes; all looking as though they were bought in different decades by different aunts: that bachelor look. When there's a lull in the conversation he starts mumbling. No, it's a tune. He's nervous but he doesn't care if you hear him. His hair needs cut. His sister probably does it.

There's a guy about fifty wearing the Rangers away strip, the one with the sash. He tells story after story. His targets are easy and his stories are ancient but he's funny. He's loud and animated, forceful without being overbearing. He holds court. A taxi-driver pokes his head through the door and shouts 'Taxi for Davies'. The Rangers supporter tells him there's nobody of that name in the pub. The driver repeats his request. There's no response. The Rangers supporter says, 'I told you *soooo*.' The taxi driver says 'Fuck it' and leaves.

There's a couple of lads in the corner about to fall out. They're talking and talking, interrupting each other constantly. It's to do with a woman. They look like best friends. They're not drunk or violent – they're on soft drinks – they're just upset. It was a night for sorting things out but it hasn't worked. Tears will flow rather than blood.

There's a really old couple talking to each other. He's wearing his best suit, she's got her hair nice and her jewellery on. They talk about entirely different subjects. He's on about the old days at the pictures when the audience used to do turns on stage between the features, and she's on about a holiday they had in Blackpool during the war but she can't remember what year it was.

The Rangers supporter shouts 'WHOAH-HO!!! You not dead yet, you old cunt? By God, you fucking look it, sir.'

The old guy who's just entered the bar stops in his stride. He looks disgusted, as if someone's spat in his soup. He's so old he'd look dead even if he was healthy. And he looks anything but healthy, more like an ex-kamikaze pilot that did overtime. But he's got a good head of black hair and a leanness which suggests he was once a fine looking young man. He shouts 'FUCKING ORANGING CUNTING BASTARD!' and sprays everyone within a ten-yard radius. The Rangers supporter asks who won the league. 'A shower of fucking English poofs and their fucking uncles, the referees.' The old guy goes on to quote examples and condemn the guilty.

There's a couple. He looks like he used to hang around with nutters with his tattoos and boxer's build. He's got a side-shed and his hair's greasy. His hands clasp his spread knees, showing the veins on his forearms. She looks twenty-six. She's wearing a thin leather jacket and snow-washed jeans. Her knees together, she leans forward when she flicks her cigarette, as though over-anxious not to miss the ashtray. Everybody stops and talks with them – about families, betting and work – but nobody ever sits beside them.

A young lad comes in. He's stoned out his crate, brain dead and body irrelative. He pushes his hand through his hair but he doesn't need to. It's too short to be out of place. He asks for a packet of cigarette papers. The barmaid shakes her head. No. The bar falls silent. She looks like your favourite auntie. The lad looks lost. The bar starts sniggering. The barmaid gives him his cigarette papers. She says, 'Here you are then. You'll be needing something to roll your hash in. Eh, son?' The lad straightens up and exits rapidly, red-faced, as everyone bursts out laughing at him.

The old guy and the Rangers supporter get back to arguing. The greatest footballer of all time. It's George Connelly versus Jim Baxter. They recall passes, dribbles, goals and the opinions of others. They point out similarities and revel in differences. It looks like the Rangers supporter's taking the piss out the old guy, but it isn't like that. The old guy gives as good as he gets. He's fucking vicious.

There's the alcoholic and her husband. She drinks fast, really fast. She tells of how wrecked she's been and about the DTs and the blackouts. She's incredibly sexy and touches everyone, grabbing them and stroking them. Her hands are shaking and she says, 'Look at this!' She says, 'What was I like, Tam? Tell them what I was like,' but she never lets anybody get a word in.

There's a guy that looks as if he's English, as if he plays golf with Des Lynam. He's wearing glasses and a yellow V-neck jumper. He drinks shorts and pints. There's five of them but he dominates. They look like managers or foremen. They speak of others using surnames: 'I told Harris . . . Johnstone's a good man . . . I'll tell you about McDonald.'

The guy who looks like a bachelor is pointing to the telly. He tells Jim to keep an eye on Alastair Burnet. He says when Alastair Burnet looks as though he's spitting, it means's he's mentioned the IRA. The guy starts humming his tune again as Jim studies the telly.

The old guy and the Rangers supporter are quizzing each other now. They start by exchanging old football jokes. Who was the only man to score past Pat Jennings with bare feet? Tony the Tiger in the *Frosties* ad. Name all the teams with x's in them? *Choo! Choo!* They rhyme off the classic sides: Real Madrid at Hampden, Brazil in '70, Leeds United at Hampden, Aberdeen in the Cup Winners' Cup final; Manchester United in '68. The pub supply questions and debate the answers. Who was the 'keeper when Willie Donachie scored his own goal? Jim Blyth. What was the highest attendance at Cliftonhill? 27,000. How old was Arthur Graham in the 1970 Cup Final? Seventeen. Who was the only English team ever to field a side made up entirely of Scots? Accrington Stanley. Who was the only second division team ever to win the Cup? East Fife. They go on and on. Everybody's got their own special question to ask. Jim asks how many goals Falkirk scored in season 35/36. The old guy says '132'. The Rangers supporter says it was the third highest total ever. The old guy says Raith Rovers had the highest and the Rangers supporter agrees. The guy who used to hang about with nutters asks what season Bo'ness United were in the first division. 'Season 27/28,' says the Rangers supporter. With a glint in his eye the old guy agrees and says they were relegated. This is serious. It's like *High Noon* without the shitty bits. The bell signals last orders but it's more like the command to come out fighting. The old guy and the Rangers supporter quiz each other about the other's team. Names fly like bullets in Beirut: Bertie Peacock, Willie Woodburn, Pat McCluskey, Iain MacDonald, Ally Dawson, Willie McStay. From where did they come and where did they go? They move from the past to the present and back again. They're naming the Cup Final sides easier than they could list their grandchildren. Games they, and tens of thousands of others, were at. They talk about matches that are twenty years old as if they took place last week. The old guy says, 'Name the side, the *classic* side, that lifted the Cup in '63?' Without thinking, the Rangers supporter rhymes off the *classic* side: 'Ritchie, Shearer, Provan, Greig, McKinnon, Baxter, Henderson, McLean, Millar, Wilson.' The old guy hollers with delight and does a jig of joy. He says, 'Fucking diddy you are, there was a replay and ...' The Rangers supporter screams 'BASTARD!' at the top of his voice while the old guy goes on to remind him of how Ian McMillan replaced George McLean in the replay. The Rangers supporter says, 'At least we won. 3–0. Destroyed you. You lot left at half-time, you were that disgusted.' The old guy concedes that that was a good Rangers side but says the reason Celtic lost was cause they bottled out of playing Jimmy Johnstone in the replay. He goes on to say Rangers were always jammy in replays and blames the referees. The old guy just won't shut up. He starts listing the Rangers sides involved in replays. He looks a bit demented and were it any other subject he would be more than whisked away in a white jacket. There's nothing *nobody* can tell him about football. The Rangers supporter threatens to empty the ice-bucket over the old guy's head if he doesn't shut up. This has the desired effect and they shake hands and agree they're both pretty smart. The Rangers supporter vows he'll one day get his revenge.

It was time to go. Jim said 'Cheerio' to the guy that looked like a bachelor and patted the old guy on the shoulder, saying, 'Well done, wee man.' The old guy turned round with his fists clenched and said, 'Hey, watch it, you. You a fucking poof or something?' Everybody laughed, Jim included, as the old guy aimed a few karate chops.

Jim fancied a fish supper but they were closing up and didn't have any fish left so he didn't bother taking anything. Outside the chip shop, a solitary young lad was in a world of his own playing keepie-uppie while waiting for his girlfriend to finish up her stint at the shop.

It was nearing midnight but Jim decided on a walk to tire himself a bit. He often wished they had a dog so as he could have an excuse to take more regular exercise, and get the stuffiness out of him. It would be a big, friendly lump, a three-tins-a-day dog. Jim also felt that something like a dog would've kept his family closer together.

His mum was all right but his sisters were cases. Pamela left home at eighteen, got married at twenty and now had two kids. She hardly speaks to her mother and didn't even turn up for her father's funeral. There are things Jim doesn't know about: namely, that while he was away at university, Pamela told her mother that her father had grabbed her breasts one night when he was drunk. It had happened before but this was the first time Pamela mentioned it to anyone. The marriage broke up soon afterwards. Their mother said that Jim shouldn't be told of the incident, so as not to affect his studying.

At twenty-seven, Lynn, Jim's other sister, is a year older than Jim. She recently moved back into the family home after being evicted from her private flat following an over-boisterous party. The police had been called in and a variety of drugs were found. Lynn was dealing speed at the time. Lynn has rows with her mother about the boyfriends she keeps. The previous week Lynn's mother had walked into her bedroom and discovered Lynn in bed with a boy from the high school. Lynn was supposed to have been at work at the time. Jim and Lynn barely talk to each other. Every comment Jim makes is interpreted as interfering. Every comment Lynn makes is intended as tease. If he didn't get off her back, Lynn was going to tell Jim what their father did to Pamela. That kind of thing's in the blood, she would say to him.

The rubbish bags were out as Jim made his way through the complex of flats. Some were untied or bursting, leaving the debris to spread over the glass-strewn pavements and onto the muddy, trampled green areas.

Jim wasn't frightened in the dark and narrow pathways. You only ever bumped into kids or old drunks. The latter just wanting to talk, to tell you their stories; referring to themselves in the third person, going on about the life they'd been lumbered with. Anyway, Jim was well known locally and believed he was regarded as an okay guy. This wasn't true. The people he regarded as friends spoke of him as being at best a curio and at worst a nuisance.

At the far end of the estate, Jim made up his mind to make his way along the banks of the burn until it reached the river then he'd get up onto the main road and head home. That would be a good walk.

Jim didn't want to leave the town, didn't want to move away. That's what a lot of his friends had done. None of them kept in touch. His remaining friends had changed completely; either married or gone off to hang around with other folk. Jim didn't think he was finished with the town. You finished something once you were successful, that's the way he saw it. He didn't want to leave and drag all that failure about with him. But instead of getting the finger out he was burying it further in. He made out he was troubled by bad memories. But these memories had to be forced and they were never graphic or shocking the way he wanted them to be. They were petty and he knew it.

He lived a life where he was being forced to do what he wanted to do. Never an easy decision. The people in the pub were happier than Ken and Katrina, that much was obvious to Jim. They fitted in. And Jim fitted in with them. And that was good enough. Living other people's lives.

Up ahead, a bridge had been formed across the burn from a smashed-up wall-unit; the drawers lay half-hidden in the undergrowth, a home for the more up-market wildlife. Jim kept sliding and getting the rips of his jeans caught so he took advantage of the bridge and crossed to the other side. As he did so, he stumbled and one of his feet sank ankle-deep into the water. Jim cursed his sopping foot. He lit a cigarette to give himself something else to think about.

The banking on this side was steeper but not so overgrown. Jim had never been this far before. He did a lot of walking but this was the furthest he'd been in ages. It was hard going and he was sweating profusely.

Just as Jim was beginning to get bored, really bored, the burn disappeared to a trickle and he found himself confronted by a dump: tons and tons and tons of rubbish, cookers, fridges and lino, chairs, mattresses and carpets, tins, cans and plastic bottles, even photographs, letters and clothes. Jim could see a dictionary, positioned as though to provide an inventory of all that could be found. It was the clothes that scared Jim as he investigated. Some were loose but most were crammed into plastic bags, taking on near-human form. Jim couldn't walk over the rubbish and he couldn't walk round it cause the banking had collapsed so he had to go up. It wasn't easy and he twisted his ankle as he climbed. Eventually he made it over the new fence and on to the road.

From here Jim could see the full extent of the mess and just how far down he'd been. On the far side of the dump there were half a dozen large industrial drums and what appeared to be hundreds of small tins. Some of them were trapped in a bush at the top of the bank. Jim went over to get a closer look. They were dog-food tins.

Jim turned homeward and could see the flames and the smoke of the industry. The constant humming and irregular clanging were more noticeable than in the daytime, the noxious smells more imposing. Jim could pick out four or five different smells, as distinct as the voices in a pub. It was home and it was where he wanted to be. Nobody ever said it had to be pretty. And what was the point if it was?

As he headed back Jim passed the 'No Dumping' sign. Somebody had changed the D to an H. Jim laughed out loud. He noticed that there was a swing that could take you high above the dump. He supposed the kids came up here on their bikes and used it. When he was a kid, Jim had done things like that. Dangerous things.

For the early part the walk back was all very up and down and very tiring. It seemed ages before the ground levelled to a steady, shallow downhill and Jim could hear traffic and saw puddles of broken glass at the side of the road. He figured he couldn't have far to go.

If you'd have seen him, you'd have seen a guy walking with a limp and smoking a cigarette. He was wearing a horrible ski jacket, torn and dirty jeans and crappy trainers he'd bought for £3.99. Somebody who'd spent the early evening seeing some old friends then visiting a friendly pub. But that hadn't been enough. Even now he would read or watch television when he got home.

Jim stopped at the all-night garage for more cigarettes. The door was locked and the old guy was just serving from the window. Only the taxi drivers were being allowed in. Jim asked what was going on and the old guy explained how he'd been attacked last week. He asked was there anything Jim was wanting, like. Jim thought for a second and decided on a chilli-beanburger. The old guy put one in the microwave and said it would be ready in a minute. Jim asked how the snooker had been going and they talked about the snooker until the burger was ready. Jim was conscious of the taxi drivers giving him the once-over.

While they were talking, a car full of lads drove in at speed, searching out supplies for the night's partying. Jim heard them asking for cigarettes, cigarette papers, and juice. There was a big debate as to what munchies they should get. It dawned on Jim he'd bought twenty cigarettes when he'd only intended getting ten. That was him skint now. He'd need to get a sub off his mum to do him till his next giro.

Jim ate his burger as he made his way through the flats. A few of the lights were on and would remain so. People like Jim who had no reason to rise early so they stayed up late, partying and watching TV or videos.

Jim crossed the bridge that led to the four-in-a-block estate and tossed his food packaging into the burn. Something in the water caught his eye. It was the doll he'd seen earlier. Jim recalled another baby. Something he'd forgotten about. About an old school friend called David Jones – the lad they called Bowie. He'd got a girl pregnant and immediately his folks upped and moved to the borders. The girl had dumped the baby at this bridge when it was born.

A shout from the four-in-a-block startled Jim. Still kneeling, he turned his head to see a young girl running down the road. She was about fourteen or so and wore only a loosely tied dressing-gown. Jim watched her flashing white legs as she ran. It was quite beautiful. He felt anxious for her. The girl stopped running and bent over with her hands on her knees. She started laughing and pointed back in the direction in which she had come from. Jim followed her finger. He saw a big, hefty woman with arms folded against the cold and slippers flapping as she walked. The woman caught up with the girl and they put their arms around each other's shoulders and entered one of the houses.

A dizziness came over Jim as he stood up. He closed his eyes and he could see something moving really fast, like a wheel or a roulette table. If he concentrated he could see faces round the rim. All the faces were pleased to see him. Asking for him. Politely so. All that is apart from his mother and his sisters who stared out accusingly as if something was his fault.

Jim turned to the flats. He seen Ken and Katrina's bathroom light was on. He didn't know what he wanted from Katrina. He didn't love her. He tried to tell himself that he loved her, but he didn't. He felt it would make him a better person to love someone. No, a more complete person. Normal. Now she made him feel awkward. Jim assumed that since they'd known each other for so long then their friendship would always be more personal, special and somehow empathic.

While Jim was down there with the litter and his thoughts, Katrina washed her face with cold water. Earlier on they talked of parties and Katrina mentioned that she'd only once been 'upstairs' at a party. She'd been very young and very drunk and the man she was with had raped her. It had been the first time. She woke up the following morning with bruises on her inner thighs and wrists. Hating herself, she became sick from the alcohol, and sick and sore from the sex. Over the years she'd managed to live with the incident and become relaxed with men. But tonight that horrible smug grin on Jim's face had upset her. *That smirk.* Surely to God, Jim of all people hadn't forgotten how much that night had distressed her and the effect it had on her growing up?

Katrina was assuming Jim knew what happened that night. That somebody had told him. But – like so many things in his life – the facts of the matter and its consequences were unknown to him.

Kevin

Gary! Gary!

Yeah, through here. What is it?

Gary, there's a broken bird out front. Could you fix it for us?

What's wrong with it?

Its wing's broken and it isn't moving.

Not at all?

No.

Well, if it isn't moving, there's not much chance of being able to fix it.

How not?

Cause if it's not moving – it's dead.

Kevin could fix it.

Your mam said you were on about this Kevin yesterday. Who's he? Does he stay in the private houses?

No. Mrs Johnson knows him.

What, the jannie?

No.

. . .

. . .

Where is the bird?

Next to Tam and Alison's lock-up. Andrea's watching it.

Okay, let's go and have a look. Hold on, I better lock the door. You know what your mam's like about us leaving it unlocked.

Hurry up.

All right, I'm coming. What happened to the bird? Do you know?

No. Andrea said it was there yesterday. There it is.

Well, I'm afraid there's nothing I can do – the bird is dead.

Kevin could fix it. We'll take it to school.

No. It's dead, son. Nothing anybody can do for it.

Kevin could. Mrs Johnson said he fixes everyone.

I doubt it. No, leave it. Don't touch it. It's dirty. I'll put it in the bucket.

No. We'll wrap him up and take him to Kevin.

Right. Once and for all, who is this Kevin? How did you hear about him?

Mrs Johnson told us about him.

What did she say?

She said that when Jesus died he went away to Kevin, and Kevin fixed him, so he could come back again.

I Don't Go Round There Anymore

Not so long ago there was a period when I was round there all the time. That's when I had major money problems and I got my electricity cut off. I knew when I went there I would get fags and I would get to see the paper, it would be warm and I would get food. I was selfish when I went there. Rotten, really. I used them.

I was never a close friend. They weren't people I grew up with, or went to football with or went to gigs with. We never talked about football or records. That's normally all I ever talk about.

Their folks are wealthy. They've got enough crystal to fill a shop window and the most expensive suite I'll probably ever sit on. The father does a lot of contract work. He's spent time in the Middle East and in the Falklands. Presently he's earning ludicrous amounts of money working on the Channel Tunnel. Him and his wife were really good to me. They got my name wrong on more than a few occasions but that was part of the appeal. Believe me, at the time it was comforting to be anonymous.

There was also a sister – whom, incidentally, I used to fancy a wee bit – but she was nothing like them and left early on. 'Them' being the three brothers: John, Tim and Peter. They still live at home.

John will die within the next few years unless he stops drinking. I remember him from school as being quiet and one of the few smokers that wasn't a nutter. Following school we started working together and on Friday nights the pair of us would go out and get completely rat-arsed. When I lost my job he quite often treated me. It wasn't just the Friday nights he went out, though. Then there was the trouble with Marion. Then he jacked his job in. It wasn't long till he was drinking during the day every day. Socially at first then always on his own. The house and the car would conceal cans planted every-where. It was funny in the old days, hiding them from his folks ('I'm just away out to see the car') but when he searched for cans that weren't there you had to start questioning things. It was like looking through all your pockets knowing there must be money somewhere, not believing you'd spent it all.

All John's theories and stories about life were lent a sensitivity which drew you to him. It wasn't the brutal honesty of his failures so much as the fear that got to me. The fear of his problem. I read a James Ellroy book called *Brown's Requiem* about this private eye who would call on his alcoholic friend, Walter, when he had a lot on his mind and cause he cared about the guy. Sometimes the guy would be brilliant (he saw nothing but the facts) and sometimes he was best left alone (he saw nothing but his facts). That was a bit like me and John. He helped me out when I had my money problems. It was straight-forward for him. He just said, 'Here you are. Saves me spending it on drink.' Latterly, though, there was little clarity and communication became almost negligible. Just inward-ness and, I have to say, paranoia. I was way past the stage of seeing nothing but self-pity and realized just how ill the guy was. You read and hear a lot about celebrity alcoholics and their binges – a bottle of Jack Daniels for breakfast, that kind of thing – John wasn't like that. His tolerance was low. After a few cans he would sink (plummet) into his near-unconscious sleep. He spent an incredible amount of time asleep.

I actually thought getting him lifted might help. I made it as far as conceiving a plan. I would plant some dope and phone the police. John would resist arrest or whatever and land himself in deep shit. He changes temper as easily as you change TV channels. I'm being serious. John is violent. His mam says he was like that in the pram; he would not sit up and he would not lie down. It's been my experience, however, that John's outbursts were always directed at objects; throwing meals, kicking doors, punching walls and breaking things. I'm sure that when he crashed the car those times it was deliberate. It gives me a strange kind of confidence to believe that, anyway.

Through John, I met Tim and got introduced to the world of dope. In Tim's bedroom the three of us smoked our way through tons of the stuff while their mam served us up home-baked sponges, shortbread and awesome Empire biscuits. Mild panic ensued when we heard her coming up the stairs. We quickly fanned the room and closed the windows so things wouldn't look too suspicious – three guys with jackets still on watching the telly with the sound turned off. Sometimes John would drive me and Tim and another couple of guys to some quiet place – Cairnpapple, beaches on the Forth, Rannoch Moor, mushie-picking up the Braes – where we'd get pissed and stoned and we'd meditate and get confessional and pish like that. We would stay till the sun came up, then, with Tim skinning up in the back and the stereo blaring out, John would drive us home. He nearly killed us a few times – that's when we had the crashes – as he sped along those up and down bendy B roads. He loved it. We all did. We stopped the road trips when that car of his couldn't be trusted to go more than a couple of miles without breaking down.

Tim still gets (still *is*) stoned all the time. He's different from John in that he's not as personable. He's secretive and a bit, well, dodgy. There was one time when John got money from his mum to buy the week's messages. John, though, paid for the messages using a spring-loaded cheque and spent the money on a crate of beer. (None of the off-licences would accept a cheque from John.) Tim thought this was great. So for the next couple of weeks he went for the messages. Of course, he was the one that got caught. John got excused while Tim got the trouble. He gets into a lot of trouble. He got busted when he was dealing and now his folks turn away his visitors and have effectively stopped him from receiving phone calls. He's been beaten up a few times as well. For saying things he shouldn't have, for giving shoddy deals and for not paying back money. He's not overgenerous like John, though he thinks he is. His opinion of himself is almost diametrically opposed to that which people have of him.

Like John, though, Tim's come through bad experiences at work and with relationships. As far as I can gather, Tim was always at fault. The strange thing about Tim (and to a lesser extent John) is his success and popularity at parties. The casual informality and constant story-telling suit him. (Or maybe it's just that he's always got a bit of dope on him.) He's good with strangers and people who don't know him. In private conversation, though, he only perks up when there's gossip on the go. Otherwise he won't pay you one blind bit of notice. There's one Tim anecdote that might prove informative. One time he came round to see me (very unusual for him) and I was playing a record of Roxy Music's, 'Jealous Guy'. He took the record off; this was unusual in as much as he never really bothered with my records at all. He was bitter about something. You see a lot of your own worst qualities when you see someone behave like Tim. He's like something that should've been repaired ages ago but wasn't. It's not an endearing quality – but then he's not an endearing guy.

At twenty-eight, Peter is the oldest of the brothers. He lives in the same house but shares none of his brothers' excesses. Always on the go, he'd work twenty-four hours a day – or so he'd have you believe. You feel he was born when he got his first car and first job. It's surprising to the point of shocking when he makes a reference to his schooldays. It's like your dad talking about school. The least bright (and also least pretentious) of the three, his lack of intelligence is disturbing. I'm sorry but there's no other way to say it: the guy is thick. Thick meaning stupid and wrong. Thick meaning slow and dim. Thick meaning he'll argue with you about anything. When you watch TV with him or talk with him it can be quite embarrassing. He comes away with the most pathetic jokes, put-downs and generalizations. The guy was born to bug.

Despite the appearance of constant activity, Peter is, however, like his brothers, more commonly unemployed. While John and Tim try to con their way into taking money, Peter blatantly steals it from his folks. He never admits his crimes. That said, he's easy enough to get on with, like talking to a drunk or an ageing relative you haven't seen for a while. His brothers, though, detest him. The most lying, lazy, evil bastard under the sun, they agree. You don't know him, they say.

With most people you establish a rapport through common interests and private jokes, the brothers weren't like that. It was like talking to somebody whose mind and priorities lay elsewhere. They were polite but a little bland. They weren't daft: they never turned up the volume when a beautiful woman appeared on the telly or complained about the lack of shagging in late-night films. They weren't imposing: they never bored you with their life stories or asked you to do things for them. The fact that John *can't* work and Tim *won't* work had had a limiting effect on them. Sure, they can talk on any subject – I mean, they watch TV and videos all the time – but they talk as if from the memory of recognition not the understanding of experience or even interest.

You could say that since drink and drugs are great then why shouldn't John and Tim live that way? But for them things aren't that great and never have been. They were only ever hangers-on socially (never part of a team) and now they've dropped off. For the brothers, it was all they were left with, cause it was all they ever had, and it turned into a dogma. When I think of John, I think of drink, and when I think of Tim, I think of dope. There were no careers, no relationships, nothing worth mentioning.

Tim can get a bit macho about drugs; how he's done this and how he's done that. He did mushies for the first time when he was thirteen and he claims to have freebased cocaine with a couple of guys through in Glasgow 'years ago'. I've seen him on the mushies. He's totally bottled up. He looks wild, manic. He doesn't appear to be enjoying it at all. Tim loves telling of the time we all did acid and went to Bo'ness Fair and I freaked out on the rib-tickler. While he's telling others about this, he's staring at me. He doesn't tell it as a story, he states it as a fact. Some people could make things like that funny. Tim can't or won't.

One day Big Duncan came round to see me and we got to talking about them. Slagging them off for never paying dig money. That always bugged me. Duncan knows them from way back and gave up hope for them years ago. He pointed out it wasn't always the case that they swore at their parents, same with the fighting. Just these past five years, he said matter-of-factly. That's when all the breakages and bruises started. It used to be they would storm off (John even 'ran away'), now they stay and fight. It's fear again. Fear of storming off cause they've nowhere to go. It's the swearing I hate. Peter's the worst. Swearing at his mam. Crude, really crude. She was always Roseanne, the smart-arse who could make you laugh while getting her own way. I really admired that woman. The last I heard she was in hospital.

I started to wonder why I continued to go round there. Nobody else went there anymore. I was worried I was going for voyeuristic reasons. It's good stuff, too. Adopt any stance with pleasure. Make it funny – dry, black, laconic, tragi-comic – and, hey, you've got top-flight entertainment! But I've looked through all my notes and thought through all my thoughts and I find no reference to them. And do you know why? Well, it's cause they were boring bastards. I've never fallen out with any of them cause I was never really close to any of them. As I said, I used them.

I used them in ways they don't even know about.

I mentioned that John had trouble with a girl called Marion. Marion spent a couple of nights at my flat. John doesn't know about this. She had an argument with him one night and she came round here. I told her she was best to finish with him cause he was a drunken bum. It wasn't long before she agreed with me and we had a couple of good nights together. One of the times Peter was blamed for stealing money was down to me as well. I stole a tenner cause I fancied a donar kebab and some pakora. I knew I'd get away with it. I went round there cause I didn't have any fags and cause I got my electricity cut off. John's the only person in the world I owe money to. In terms of fags I owe him Embassy UK Limited.

I'm getting married soon and they say they're pleased for me. Everybody says I shouldn't invite them. They'll cause trouble I'm told. They'll be embarrassing. Our lot look down on them. The mention of their names can make us laugh: we laugh at their clothes and what we've done to avoid bumping into them in the street. Nobody likes them. Really, I don't think they would be embarrassing. They come from a massive family. They're used to these kind of get-togethers. As I said, they were good at parties. Still, I won't invite them. I'd like Anne-Marie to meet them, though. I'll maybe do something about that. I'm not ashamed of them.

In that house, just now, every door is open and every heater's on full blast; the phone's ringing and there's someone at the back door; every ashtray's overflowing and there's mugs and dishes all over the place; the father's in the garage (he couldn't handle the Channel Tunnel – the wages were exaggerated and they treated the men like shite); the mother's in the kitchen making herself a coffee; and Peter's watching television, Tim's skinning up and John's crashed out. There's also a dog, two cats, a fish tank and an obnoxious parrot.

I remember a Christmas when I was soaking and thoroughly miserable until I plucked up enough courage to go round there. I discovered grannies, grandads, aunts, uncles, cousins and kids having a great time and getting absolutely plastered. It was the best Christmas I ever had.

If I went round just now there's a chance I'd enjoy myself. Get to hear all the local gossip and get tons of food. It's more likely, though, that I'd feel awkward and wonder what the fuck I was doing there. Either way, I have no intention of finding out.

Life on a Scottish Council Estate
Vol. I Chap. 3

So I've got a new flat and the good news is there are two spare bedrooms (one for the Scalectrix, one for the shagging) – but the bad news is it's the lowest of the low on the difficult to let list in the heart of Dodgy Cunt City wherein my neighbours look like the cast of *The Name of the Rose* with tattoos, and the kids come to my door, shout, 'KILL THE WILLY!' then punch me in the balls and run away. This close is wild, man; even a dog called Bongo doesn't come on round here . . . Anyway, there's a knock at the door. It's the post with a package from my pal Mikey in London. My pal Mikey's wrote me a letter and sent me a tape of the Stone Roses and Happy Mondays. He says I'm going to love this tape. He says I've got to give it twenty listens cause it's one of those – growers. He tells me we've got to get hold of ecstasy. He says it's the greatest drug of all time. Eh? Now my pal Mikey's pretty much like myself, a records/football/shagging man, and for him to be raving about a drug is pretty much akin to my grannie raving about drugs! . . . Edwyn, English Edgar and The Tank come round. I tell them the news and play them the tape . . . We're into it. The Tank says, 'That boy's some guitarist.' (The Tank says things like that.) Edwyn and English Edgar take it upon themselves to contact The Big Man and get him to organize the ecstasy. They set out on their mission. Wee Harry comes round. He's jacked in his job, he's left Wendy and he's just botched up an attempt at slashing his wrists. No problem, we tell him. Party, the night, my bit, be here. Ecstasy, we tell him. My pal Mikey's raving about it. Wee Harry says it's his last hope. He leaves to tell Wendy. Hamish arrives. He doesn't have any money but he wants an ecstasy. We tell him he's got till The Big Man arrives. Can Hamish do it? Time will tell. Stuart is next. 'Party?' he asks. *Party,* we tell him. He's got a new jumper and a wee bit of dope. The Tank tells him to save the dope till later. Stuart is distraught again. The more people present the less he'll get. We wait . . . . we're waiting . . . . waiting for the Big Man. Stuart's staring at his wee bit of dope, The Tank's fast-forwarding a Michelle Pfeiffer video to get to the shagging bits and I'm making coffee. The door goes. It's Carmel. She says she wants an ecstasy. She's heard it makes you horny. This is incredible! If Carmel gets any hornier the paint'll come off the walls. Carmel is a primary school teacher in real life. Wee Harry and Wendy arrive. They're together but they're not talking to each other. I politely ask them not to smash my windows or my hi-fi and not to throw any records at each other. The door goes yet again! It's Grant and Wee Harry's wee sister. This is their first night out together. The air of tension and expectancy is incredible. We're waiting . . . . we're standing about like workies . . . . waiting for The Big Man. ' I RECOGNIZE THAT KNOCK' we all scream at once – but it's only Edwyn and English Edgar pretending to be The Big Man. Edwyn's been on his uncle's phone and fax machine all day and everything's set. The Big Man is due. Piggy banks have been raided, accounts have been overdrawn and families have been borrowed from. There's an apologetic knock at the door. 'Oh no, he couldn't get any,' we all groan at once. But it isn't The Big Man . . . *it's my psychotic big brother!* He says, 'Hello, Gordon.' I say, 'Hu-hu-hu-hu!' He asks if he can come in. I let him in cause he's wearing flares, a hooded top and hundred-and-twenty quid Reeboks. Something is very strange. He tells me he's stopped drinking and tells me that he loves me. This is all very emotional and all very weird. He's never embraced me – he's only ever hit me. He says 'Hello' to everybody and asks what's happening. I tell him we're waiting for The Big Man bringing up the ecstasy. 'Brilliant,' he says. He says he did tons of the stuff when he was in prison. My *ex*-psychotic big brother goes on to say that there's at least three hundred places in Glasgow manufacturing ecstasy. (Really, and I thought all they did was walk greyhounds.) He says a lot of it's bad, though, and a lot of it's dodgy. (That's more like Glasgow.) We tell him The Big Man'll get us good stuff. 'Good,' he says and tell us he's got a couple of acid-house tapes in his bum-bag. *(He's wearing a bum-bag!)* They'll do for later on, he tells us. We wait . . . . there is no more exciting place in the world to be the night than my bit . . . . the guy who's going to be shagging Madonna is bored out of his skull by comparison . . . . we're waiting for The Big Man. Outside I hear a car tooting its horn. I RECOGNIZE THAT TUNE. IT'S THE BIG MAN! I rush to the door and let him in. He's got a taxi here straight from the airport. *Prestwick airport!* He's got the ecstasy, enough for everybody. 'You call them E's,' my ex-psychotic big brother tells me. The Big Man says they're good ones. My ex-psychotic big brother says they look good. They look like aspirins to the rest of us. The Big Man says he got them off one of his fellow pilots. He says all the pilots are 'on one'. You call it being 'on one' my ex-psychotic big brother tells us. Wendy asks if it's like acid/mushies/speed. The Big Man says, 'No/No/ No.' We all breathe a sigh of relief because we don't want to end up like Stuart. 'There's no paranoia,' says my ex-psychotic big brother, who, like most nutters, used to be pretty moralistic about drugs. He says it isn't crude and the comedown's beautiful. The Big Man says he could do with a smoke of dope. We tell him all we've got is Stuart's wee bit. 'Pity,' says the Big Man – then he looks round him, like we're on a mission or something, and says, 'Okay. Let's drop the E's.' We wait . . . . we're waiting . . . . we're waiting to see what happens. There's a knock at the door. It's two sixteen-year-olds the size of giants in police uniforms. They ask to be let in. I let them in. They ask me to turn down my music. I turn down my music. They eye my visitors. My visitors smile back. They ask my name, my date of birth and how old I am. I'm really polite and cool and tell them. All of a sudden The Tank says, *'Fucking hell, man'* and planks himself down in the corner. He looks like Buddha doing an impression of Yogi Bear. Wee Harry starts dancing to the Happy Mondays. Really dancing, like an African. *Wee Harry never dances!* He listens to Gustav Mahler and *Leonard Cohen Sings Peter Hammil* and reads Sylvia Plath for breakfast. Edwyn and English Edgar ask if they can go through to my spare bedroom. 'Just for a minute,' they say. *They never ask!* They usually just disappear. Wendy and Grant and Wee Harry's wee sister start dancing with Wee Harry. *Really dancing!* Carmel's running her fingers through her hair and moaning gently. *The paint is seriously coming off the fucking walls, man.* She's so into herself, it's unreal. The Big Man says, 'Yeah, I'm well into this' and sits himself down beside The Tank and gives him a cuddle. The last time I seen that grin on his face was when he got the love-bites from Wee Jeannie Wright on the school trip to Switzerland. Stuart looks cool. As if he's savouring something. *Stuart looks cool!* Stuart never looks cool. *Never, never, never.* He's sitting two feet from two policemen, he's got dope secreted about his person and he's looking cool. Like he's normal or something. My ex-psychotic big brother is going round asking everybody if they're all right. He asks the policemen if they're all right. The police don't look all right. They're filling their notebooks. I turn the tape over. This is my twentieth listening of The Stone Roses LP – *fucking godlike.* I'm grinding my teeth and I'm telling the police The Stone Roses are fucking godlike. The police note this down then leave. I see them to the door. Me, I like the police. They lock up nutters. More power to them. I watch their car leave the court then rush back to my living-room and turn up my music. Stuart skins up his dope. Edwyn and English Edgar reappear. They now wish to be known as The E Boys. Wee Harry and Wendy head off to the spare bedroom. They're best pals again. There's a knock at the door. It's Hamish. He asks, 'Was that the feds?' I tell him it was but everything's cool. I ask if he got the money all right. He says, 'You're not going to believe this but I've just won on the big bandit up the club. I'm fucking loaded. Fucking hell,' he says when he sees everybody. *'Give me some!'* Everybody is pleased to see Hamish. Everybody loves Hamish. *Eh?* The Big Man asks if Hamish has any dope. Hamish tosses a lump over to The Big Man then he does his Blue Peter and removes a two-foot-long joint from his coat pocket and says, 'And here's one I prepared earlier.' I ask Carmel how she's doing. She says she thought she'd feel really horny but the only person she's into is herself. Pity, I says to myself. She starts that moaning again. *She's glowing, man. She's glowing.* Every breath brings it back on. Wee Harry reappears. He's wearing only his Ys and announces emphatically, 'I understand the sixties! This stuff is important!' That's all he says, then heads back through to my spare bedroom. There is a wonderful atmosphere. Everything's worked out all right. Nobody's fighting or falling out or being sarky. *Why? . . . Ecstasy?* My ex-psychotic big brother points to The Tank, The Big Man, Hamish and Stuart (who are passing round the big joint) and says, 'That's called chilling out.' He points to Grant, Wee Harry's wee sister, Carmel and The E Boys (who are dancing) and says, 'That's called vibing out.' I cuddle my ex-psychotic big brother and he says, 'And this is what it's all about.'

(to be continued)

I Never Thought It Would Be You

Sharon gets merry and talks gibberish when she's stoned. Me, I just get mellow and sluggish. So I wasn't really giving her what you'd call my undivided attention until she kissed me on the cheek and said, 'I never thought it would be you, that's for sure.' I asked what she was on about but she just said 'You know' like it was a question or something. From the glint in her eye, I suspect she was talking about us.

We scored our dope earlier on round at Colin's. Sharon doesn't like Colin or that lot – and they don't like her. She's a funny person, not a fun person, kind of privately witty as opposed to the more publicly wanton (i.e. thick) types they go for. Anyway, Colin had a crowd of them in and my attention was drawn to a rather plump girl taking in a massive blast from Colin's hookah pipe. (Identical to the one in *Raiders of the Lost Ark*, Colin never tires of telling folk.) She was well gone and didn't recognize me or my name. I recognized her, though, and could put a name to her, no problem. You see the girl in question was my first-ever proper girlfriend. My childhood sweetheart. She was there with some English guy from over the old town she now lives with. To be honest, she looked a bit silly. She had on those really tight ski-pants (which she had to keep pulling up), high heels and a baggy, hooped top which kept sliding down to reveal her flesh-coloured bra-straps. Like a lot of the women round here she was wee, fat and dumpy with that short, uninteresting hair more suited to the older generation.

It was pointless us staying since they were all so out of it, so basically we just said, 'Hello/How you doing?/See you soon/ Cheerio'. Sharon wouldn't go within a mile of that pipe, anyway.

On our way home, Sharon said the girl on the pipe could have been quite pretty if she'd learn how to put her lips together right. Sharon says things like that. She picks out flaws in people and renames them accordingly. My childhood sweetheart is now immortalised as squintlips.

This is my longest relationship and only the first time I've lived with someone. I was engaged when I was seventeen but – to tell the truth – it was something you did when you were that age; like taking driving lessons or visiting lots of different pubs. All these previous relationships ended with me storming off. I made out that I just wanted to party all the time but that wasn't the truth. It would be truer to say I never felt I was being shown enough affection. I was always anxious for company but once I'd secured it, it never seemed to satisfy. The chase had been more satisfying. When I said 'I love you' I was begging a response. It's different now. No, *I'm* different now. Before, I'd have gone off and shagged someone else and that would have been the end of it. Not now. For once I've seen something through. I've stuck with something and I like what it's become. Those three little words are now said with a smile. Like laughter, they express a reaction. I'm comfortable with that distance that sometimes comes between us. I'm comfortable with silence, too. Never used to be. But then I used to be terrified of spiders.

We've both lived here all our lives and we'd known each other for years before we got together. I guess that's what she meant by 'I never thought it would be you'. She was the trophy and I was the winner.

Life with my childhood sweetheart was somewhat different, and, in retrospect, somewhat prophetic. She stayed over the back and we got each other to and from school, spent the evenings together then sent coded messages at bedtime using the venetian blinds. We were in and out of each other's houses all the time, just coming and going as we pleased. I got treated like her brother when I went there. That means I got crisps and helped myself to juice. It also means I got rows and had to help with the washing-up.

On Saturday mornings we went to the old ice-rink. My skates doubled as weapons, ready to slash anybody that acted out of turn. I used to spend hours in front of the mirror, fantasising about protecting old squintlips. She was the one who told me that if she stuck her tongue in my mouth I'd get a hard-on. A point I took great pleasure in her proving. We split up soon afterwards cause she wouldn't let me shag her. (That's the prophetic bit.)

I started hanging about with my brothers and their mates. They were older and they smoked and played some fairly serious games of football on the school pitch at night. Following one of these games I got to shag one of our groupies, Lynn 'Bucket' Sommerville, in the kiddies pipe round the back of Connery Place on a night when the rain just pissed down. I wasn't the first person to have done this – but if she kept records I was probably the quickest. I should have been more patient with old squintlips.

Me and Sharon have had a few problems recently. Most of them come from me: my friends and my family. They're not friends really, just guys from work I go out to get rubbered with. Guys whose wives are called 'her' and who spend their time and wages in pubs. Going out for a drink with them means you get well blottoed and you spend a fair bit of money. The other night me and Sharon had a verbal set-to on account of me blowing forty quid in an afternoon drinking session. I tried to explain that sometimes I have this incredible desire just to forget about everything and get absolutely wrecked. (This comes about the sixth pint. The pint of no return. Sorry.) I'm slow to think and clumsy when I talk so this came out sounding like me saying that the money that went on the house was her money and that I was entitled to the occasional after-noon out. I say some pretty stupid things when I argue with Sharon. I always end up sounding holier than thou. The trouble is I like getting pissed. I feel I talk a lot of sense when I'm pissed. There's this Chinese boy I know who talks perfect English after six pints of Guinness, that's kind of the way I see myself. I know it wouldn't be the end of the world if I gave up those afternoon sessions with the boys from the work – I mean, forty quid – and I know it's all acting, hamming it up with the lads, but I like that. I've always done it. I thought I always would.

Sometimes I take this home with me and I'll go, 'The trouble with you is . . . It's about time you . . . you . . . you . . . you . . .'. Sharon swallows and says, 'Okay then.' Then she pretends to go off in the huff. There is no such thing as Sharon letting me win an argument. What she's doing is biding her time, cause you can bet your bottom dollar that she'll come back with one of her perfect, sarky comments. As I said, she's funny, not fun, she's also a piss-taker rather than a ball-breaker. She knows I'll open my mouth and make a complete cunt of myself. Her favourite put-down is to remind me that I have no sense of smell. It works as sarcasm and it hurts.

Our families don't help. That's her sisters and my brothers: her Diane and her Peggy and my Andrew and my Martin. Her sisters are doing well – my brothers should be doing time. She visits her lot and goes shopping – my lot come round to cadge fags and money. They've stolen from here. Stole twenty quid once. They pleaded their innocence, of course, knowing that I would stick up for them. Brother that I am, I duly did. But when things returned to normal I took them aside and told them if it ever happened again I would take their noses off. I was quite proud of myself. I meant it. My brothers can be tiresome. They go on about the trouble they've been in and the women they've been seeing. This leads them onto stories from the past involving me. Sharon doesn't bother about these stories. She's got a broad back and dismisses my brothers in terms of smell – Andrew of ammonia and Martin of methane. They don't get it. My brothers used to come away with stories concerning Sharon. Who she'd been out with and what happened, that kind of thing. At first they bothered me but not anymore. I'm glad there were others before me. Maybe that's what she meant by 'I never thought it would be you'. She was the booby prize and I was the lumber.

Sharon's sisters don't care much for me. One of them told me as much when she said all men treated all women like shit. Like, you're excused, you can't help being a man. Actually, her sisters and me get on all right. It's friendly banter mostly. They're really protective of her. She's the baby of the family. She doesn't tell them she smokes dope, although I suspect they know. They're not stupid.

I don't know whether that's true about all men treating all women like shit. I'm trying to think of examples that contradict and I'm struggling. My dad? No. My friends? Mmmmm some. Only some. Guys from work? No. My brothers? Case proved. Me? . . . No, until recently. Yeah, until Sharon. She'd disagree. She'd laugh at that. What generalisations can you make about women? Moody.

I like her when she's like this. Normally she doesn't fit in too well with my world. Like in pubs or at gigs she gets bored quickly and invents a headache so we have to leave. I'm not bothered. If she's not happy we're as well not being there. And as for getting her to come and watch me playing in the summer league – eh, that's a non-starter. But she likes her wee bit of blow does Sharon.

I encourage her to smoke dope because all the couples I know that smoke together stay together. They have stable, long-term relationships. They function as a team. You think of them in those terms. Maybe it's just the people I know, but that's the way I see things. That's what I aspire to.

If that sounds a bit desperate then maybe I am. Sharon's taken to this and I'll go along with it. I don't get the same hit as her, though, I'm not relaxed, I'm agitated. Anyway, that's my problem. It's not something we talk about.

The best nights out we have (and, I believe, the best nights out anybody could have) are when we take our wee bit dope round to Keith's and Ruth's. We try to time our visits to coincide with those of Eddie and Jane. Keith and Eddie are brilliant when they get going. They tell their stories from when they used to have the band, and they had their mild flirtation with fame. It's the same stories every time we see them but what the hell. Sharon loves those nights out. She laughs till she's sore.

Sharon said, 'I never thought it would be you.' I was thinking I couldn't say that because it's too glib. There's a whiff of disappointment in there as well. Women are like that. They specialise in rabbiting on for hours about nothing in particular, then out of the blue comes something that does your head in. It keeps you on your toes.

But, as I'm sure she would point out, I'm clumsy and I don't have a sense of smell. I forgot she kissed me when she said it. No, I didn't forget. It's just that that wasn't where I'd put the emphasis. Actions speak louder than words. That's one of hers. Especially when I'm drunk. It's worth thinking about. It's worth remembering.

At Last, A Story About My Bike

This story comes from the time I cycled down to London to see Falkirk playing Glasgow United in the European Cup Final. (Glasgow United being formed from the merger of Celtic and Rangers to challenge the all-conquering George D. Long-managed Bairns. The union of these great (sic) clubs followed the disclosure that the entire Celtic board were also members of the Masonic Lodge.) Anyway, Falkirk were going for three-in-a-row while Glasgow United had qualified as domestic league champions (with every single referee on their payroll, I might add).

My bicycle came in handy since Napalm Death were playing Wembley arena that self-same night so I could bomb over there once the football had finished. I'd miss none of the analysis of the game or the build-up for the gig cause I had a portable TV in my handlebar-bag and Radio Peel was broadcasting a special from the arena. It was the greatest night of my life. My wee brother bagged a couple as Falkirk won 8-0 and the Napalms were back to their brilliant best.

After leaving the arena I stopped and did a piss by the statue of Alf Ramsey as a mark of disrespect and cause I was needing a piss. But when I finished and turned round I discovered to my absolute and utter horror that my bike was gone! I couldn't believe it. I'd had it locked up and everything. Now I have nightmares about flat tyres at the best of times but this was too much. I was in tears. I thought about Paul McStay's second own goal to cheer myself up but it didn't work. The greatest night of my life had been ruined by the disappearance of my best and greatest friend. Things like this don't generally happen to me and I must admit I didn't handle it well. I was howling and hammering the ground with my fist and screaming all manner of obscenities when a couple of passing policemen noticed my plight and asked me what was wrong. As if to make things worse they assumed I was a despairing Glasgow United supporter. Indignantly, I informed them of the true nature of my grief. (Although I did leave out the bit about the piss. From previous experience I knew to my cost (£85) that London policemen wish to stamp out such activities.) The policemen were sympathetic but didn't hold out much hope for my bicycle. They were okay guys (one of them was an Arsenal supporter) and gave me a lift to a hostel they recommended.

The hostel was a gymnasium in Kentish Town. All very shiny and mirrored and bright. No one was using the facilities, everybody was just content to walk aimlessly or talk aimlessly. Those present were attired either sportily (leotards or short shorts and vests) or artily (flowing frocks or baggy suits with collar buttoned shirts or white polonecks). It was all very total trendy. I'm talking about the sort of people who go out to buy breakfast. Rich bastards. It has to be said the women were gorgeous.

I was feeling a bit out of planet when this bloke who looked incredibly like Paul Morley approached me. With a barely restrained yelp I realized that it actually and absolutely was Paul Morley! Paul fucking Morley, man: a number one hero. Wow! He came over and addressed me by name and offered me a bottle of vodka while drinking from his own. I was really starstruck. Me, I'm the sort of person who watches *The Late Show* every night just to see if he's going to be on it. Morley explained without preamble that the disappearance of my bicycle was no mere petty theft but an act of political sabotage carried out by a group of what he termed 'anarcho-leftist bullshitters'. He showed me a picture of their leader. Mega-yeuchs, man! The poor guy's face was shaped in such a manner that you felt it should have been green. It was leading anarcho-journalist-ranting poet, Steven Wells. Morley said that the difference between the two had reached the point where acts of terrorism were now commonplace. I was bewildered. I asked what the fuck he was going on about. Morley blew air in a chuckling sort of fashion, shook his head and declared, 'Beer and vodka.' None the wiser, I was now bamboozled (hic). But my confidence in the presence of the great man was growing so I asked what all this had to do with my (teetotal) bicycle. Morley sucked air this time and looked at me as if I was really thick. Not really thick in the way that I supported Glasgow United, but really thick in the way that I'd never heard of Glasgow United! I was hurt. It seemed that me and my bicycle weren't that important.

Morley left me to go to talk to some guy I'm sure I should've recognized but didn't. I wandered around. Morley had been disappointing, vague and without any semblance of passion. I'd dig him up for that when I saw him again. He actually looked as if he liked this place. I didn't. It wasn't my kind of hostel. I'm more used to being surrounded by 'interesting' Australians and sexy wee continentals wanting to practise their English out on me.

Now this always happens, but whenever I think of sex, I think of sex again. The reason for this was the encroachment upon my presence by a popular newsreader of the day. Now this was a woman I fancied something rotten. She smiled seductively then suggested I should change my clothes, saying the vest and short shorts combination would best show off my fine, lithe body. (It was the way she said it, like.) She was in a leotard. She looked so much younger and smaller. Her legs were amazing, man. My fantasies and reality were the thickness of a ball-hair from becoming one. Not only did I fancy her but I seriously fancied my chances. The popular newsreader said I looked hungry and gave me directions to the café. She said she had to go and meet someone but assured me we'd meet again. I'm telling you that voice of hers would send the pope on a chugging session. I don't recall speaking during this episode.

The café served nothing but really strong coffee and shrink-wrapped tuna-mayonnaise and peanut sandwiches. They were free, though. The woman in front of me asked if I wanted any drugs. I could tell she was really into me and since I was experiencing a newsreader-induced hard-on – I said aye. She wasn't half good-looking and introduced herself as X3PH. This was something she appeared to be mighty proud of. I acted cool. Said nothing, like, and nodded only twice. Really slowly.

We retired to a bed in the corner of a big, empty dormitory. She took all the drugs and most pleasure in our coupling. So . . .

(Publisher's interruption – *Just hold on a minute, Gordon.*
How? What's up?
Look, Gordon, your books are selling like shit on a Sunday. You could do with sprucing things up.
What do you mean, like?
All this sub-Raymond Carver/quiet desperation/from the heart stuff is all well and good, but it doesn't sell. Gordon, we want a shagging scene.
Hey, it's only ugly bastards that write shagging scenes!
It's only ugly bastards that write books, Gordon. Listen, your potential as the sex symbol of British letters is out- standing. We've got to find some way of marketing you and this is it. Go for it, Gordon.
Okay, if that's what you want. But this is under artistic protest!)

Now you'll find this hard to believe, but there was a time when I was never much good at the shagging. I was never satisfied with my performance. Hell, I know this is a macho thing and all but you want to see smoke coming out the ears and nipples turning into a couple of sticks of French bread – or at least be told, 'That was really good, that.'
Then one day I was out on my bicycle . . .
I was cycling on the road to Braemar, and boy, was I struggling. I'll set the scene: gale-force winds and rain lashing down; covered in beasties of all shapes and sizes – in my hair, eyes, nose, mouth, you name it, and, as usual, when I'm in the middle of nowhere, I was desperate for food and dying for a jobby, and I was desperate for a drink and dying for a pee; not to mention the jets . . .
Fuck it, I'm going to mention the jets.
Now, the Highlands of Scotland are used as a training ground for jet-fighter pilots and, my, how the RAF love to send their wee boys out a-bobbing-and-a-weaving in and out of the

mountains. It's my understanding that they are instructed to appear from nowhere and, at twice the speed of sound, fly two feet above the heads of Falkirk-supporting, Napalm Death-loving cyclists – thereby frightening the life out of said wonderful persons. I hate those jets, man. Call me paranoid but I take it personally. I'm not alone. See when one of them (joy of joys) actually does crash, and you get the TV crews searching out a few locals for eye-witness reports, I'm telling you the old teuchters are only too willing to oblige. They can barely contain themselves as they describe the carnage with the relish of a wee boy telling you about *Robocop*.

Anyway, so I was now on the most difficult part of my climb: the Devil's Elbow. A climb so ferociously steep and soul-destroying it was named after the most evil thing anybody could think of – eh, the Devil's Elbow.

A busload of Japanese tourists passed me as I pedalled. I could hear their excitement as they found something new to film and photograph. 'Come here and look at this fucking pillock,' they said to each other in Japanese. (One day I would dearly love to go to Japan and watch them watch their home videos of holidays in Britain. They must absolutely piss themselves.)

Me, I felt like a shadow of an imitation of counterfeit shit. I wanted to go home. I'd reached the stage where I was so sore and tired I was ready to get off and walk. It was then that I discovered the secret . . .

I'd been changing gears, changing hand positions, been in the saddle, been out the saddle, leaning forward, sitting back, swinging my body, swinging my bike, every permutation under the sun, when suddenly this thing under me – which had previously exhibited something akin to a mind of its own – was responding to my impulses. Me and my bicycle were as one. I was maintaining my balance with my knees and elbows, my hands caressing (never grabbing) the handlebars as my arse pumped out the rhythm as dictated by – and this is the secret – as dictated by my calf muscles. *It's all to do with the calf muscles*. What I'd done was to think of the only part of me that wasn't in serious agony and I let my confidence stem from there. My endeavour was rewarded. I was thriving on it. Me and my bicycle ascended the Devil's Elbow as though it were some crappy wee English climb.

My facial expression changed from pain to pleasure to ecstasy. The Japanese tourists waited at the top for me. The women cheering me on while the men clamoured over each other, gaining the best vantage points to record my exertions for Japanese posterity, as I headed for the summit and ultimate climax. I'm telling you it was a cross between Alp D'Huez and Saul on the road to Damascus. I was reborn.

It was only on the long shallow downhill when I thought to myself, 'Now if I could shag like that . . .'

So now you know my secret. It's all to do with the calf muscles.

(Publisher's interruption, again – *Is that all? Gordon, apart from the bit about the French bread nipples that was absolutely shite.*

Right, can I get back to my story then?

Yeah, on you go.

Thank you very much.)

Okay. Where was I? X3PH. Ah, that's it.

Right, so I was partying with this lassie called X3PH and after an hour-and-a-half of me mastering the art of being uncomfortable she turned over and said, 'Fucking hell, man,' and then that was her totally crashed out.

I couldn't sleep. My mind wasn't into it. I was feeling guilty. I felt it was cheating on the newsreader and, to be honest, cheating on my bicycle. Maybe this sex-as-a-bicycle-substitute lark was going too far. I also felt guilty about X3PH. I was worried she was going to start getting hung up on me. She looked the type.

I returned to the gym. People were laughing now. Not because of anything funny. It just seemed the time of night when everybody started laughing. But, you know, as much as these people tried to be fun, they couldn't disguise the fact they were dull, deadly dull. I bet they didn't even know the result of the football.

I climbed a couple of flights of stairs and found myself on a verandah looking out over Kentish Town and up to Camden. While I was there Morley came up. I questioned him about my bicycle, his lack of passion and Steven Wells. He offered me another bottle of vodka. I declined. He said, 'You don't drink, do you?' I nodded and said, 'Neither does my bicycle, big-nose.' He took the hump at that and said, 'Then you'll never understand.' I shouted, 'Where's my bicycle, you?' I was mad. (Well, as mad as a mild-mannered dude gets.) Morley started giggling. I could've grabbed that nose of his and smashed him against the wall. (Yep, I was pretty mad.) Morley looked at me pleadingly and said, 'Don't you see, Wells is fat.' 'So are you,' I pointed out. And he was fat, Morley was. Not obese, but bloated. Bevvy-merchant bloated. I asked again for the where-abouts of my bicycle. Morley walked away as if there was no hope for me. He never said a word. Mind you, I don't think me mentioning his nose helped matters much.

I made up my mind to return to the dorm and get some information out of X3PH. As I was going down the stairs, I stopped on one of the landings when I heard voices coming from behind a door I would have taken to have been a cupboard. The names the voices spoke of were familiar but the voices themselves weren't. I tried the door handle but it was locked. I tried knocking but there was no response and no reaction. The voices droned on as before. This place was starting to get on my tits. I let it rest and went down and woke up X3PH. She said she'd missed me and asked me not to go away again. (Why do women say things like that when they've been asleep?) I told her I had a lot on my mind. I gave her my ultimate number one little boy lost expression. Women find this quality of mine entrancing and it gets them every time. I was breaking this lassie's heart and there was nothing I could do to stop it. I looked her in the eye and told her what I wanted was information. She nodded and when I requested she told me about Wells.

Apparently he led a group of fat women who were attempt-ing to unsettle the state through the spread of apathy and crap humour. She said they worshipped Alf Ramsey. *Something clicked*. At last, things were beginning to make some kind of sense. I asked about Morley. She said he was God. I said he used to be but like the other one his legacy was a bit dodgy at times. 'What are his intentions?' I asked. She laughed and said, 'You don't drink, do you?' I told her that was correct.

There were other things I could've asked, but that was it for me. It was time to go. I started getting my stuff together. This really hurt X3PH. She was a nice enough lassie but she couldn't undertstand there was nothing in it and that I was just using her as a bicycle substitute. She gave it her best shot and said, 'I know where your bicycle is but I'm not going to tell you unless you promise to stay.' I looked at her forlornly. See, I've got three sisters and I was brought up with all this kind of stuff so I could tell she was talking pish. She said, 'Don't go. I'll only love you more.' It didn't work. I left. You know, I think of that poor lassie sometimes and I truly hope she managed to get over me and went on to find true personal happiness.

So that was me finished with that place. There was no security so I just walked out the front door – whereupon I was to see a sight that damn near made me come in my pants. Secured to a parking meter on the other side of the road was my bicycle. It was locked with my lock and my keys were in my pocket. Now I'm a straightforward kind of bloke, never prone to showing much emotion (other than football) but I'm telling you right here and now I wept like an onion-peeler at the overtime. I cuddled and stroked my bicycle with a degree of affection which, in the eyes of some, would have seen me arrested and institutionalized. After a few minutes of this kind of stuff I got myself together and was looking forward to my pedal up the road.

Once on my bicycle I checked to see there was no traffic coming behind me and that's when I found myself staring at a group of twenty or so cyclists. They were wearing NHS specs, zipper jackets, white t-shirts with faces on them and faded Levis. They were smiling and waving at me. One was slightly older than the others but dressed the same. I waved back when I realized who it was and what he'd done. *God's classic bed-*

room victim had saved my bike. I thought about going over to say something to him but kind of figured I'd met enough heroes for one day. The sun was coming up and I had a long road ahead.

As I headed off I could quite clearly see, leaning out of a hotel window, a wee Japanese boy – couldn't have been more than five years old – with his video camera. And, you know, it's not beyond the realms of possibility that at this very moment, somebody, somewhere in Japan, is watching a video of me and Morrissey waving to each other outside a hostel in Kentish Town.

At Drink – Two Men

'See when you think of any country in the world, right – like America, France, Italy, Brazil – all you think about is shagging.'

'!!!'

'It's true – every blooming country apart from the one I was born in. And do you know why?'

'???'

'I'll tell you why – Proddies. See when you get Catholics in charge, right; they stop everybody from shagging, so everybody just wants to shag. This place, though, it's all Proddies and they stop you from drinking – so – surprise, surprise – everybody just wants to drink. *It's in the constitution, man* . . . I've been thinking about these things.'

'Well, if you ask me . . .'

'Nah, you're Scottish, there's nothing you can say.'

'So are you, wee man.'

'Nah, my grannie's Italian. I look Italian. I look like Guiseppe Gianinni with a decent haircut . . . I'm Italian.'

'Away and shite.'

'Nah, everything about me's Italian. I'm swarthy and I'm temperamental and I've got an incredibly high sex drive – that's Italian.'

'What?'

'See the Scots, right . . .'

'You hate pasta. You're the only person in the world who hates pasta.'

'Shut up. The Scots, right . . . See the Scots . . . Take for example . . . Wait a minute. I've got it. See that guy there by the cigarette machine? See the jacket he's wearing?'

'A-ha.'

'That's the sort of thing you would buy – the kind of thing Scots buy by the barrel-load – stupid-looking. The kind of thing you wear to tell the world you're crying out for help.'

'Hold on . . .'

'I mean, that's six months you've went without buying a new blue shirt. Do you ever think about trying to look cool? It's like your hair. You don't suit it short. Classic Hun-with-a-haircut look. Des from *Neighbours,* that's who you look like.'

'Everybody looks like Des from *Neighbours.* Hey, just as a matter of course, when was the last time you and your incredibly high sex drive got shagged?'

'Eighteenth of October last year. Quarter past eleven.'

'And that was a dodgy boiler if I recall right. Doesn't sound much like an incredibly high sex drive to me.'

'I know. I know. Do you know this? I haven't had a shag in the 1990s. I'm dying, man . . . Look, there's two wee lassies up at the bar, come on, let's go for them.'

'Well, eh . . .'

'See. There you go. Typical Scot. Terrified of shagging.'

'Hey . . .'

'Come on. They're wearing white mini-skirts, that means they're willing to party.'

'Jesus Christ!'

'Nah, I'm only joking. It's true, though.'

'What?'

'Whatever I was saying. The Scots don't enjoy fun. Like you, right. You've never done anything: you support a crappy first-division football team; you're in a crappy job and as for the haircut . . .'

'Hey . . .'

'It is so. Face it. Look, you've held me back, man. How come we never did anything, like formed a group or that?'

''Cause you never learned to play guitar, wee man.'

'*Me? Me?* I'm hopeless with my hands. I can't do things like that.'

'So am I.'

'But you're the clever one. The clever ones do things like that. Think about it. The singers are the cool ones, the good-looking ones.'

'You're too wee to be the singer.'

'Oh, and I suppose you think you would have had to have been the singer. You being *sooooo* sensitive, like.'

'Well, if you want to put it that way – then, yeah.'

'Look, there's a distinct difference between being fucked-up and being sensitive. It's like the way you play football; just cause you try to beat everybody doesn't mean you're any good.'

'Away and shite again. Hey, anyway, the only bands where the singers are good-looking are those shitty Glasgow bistro bands.'

'. . . FUCK OFF! . . .'

'They all look Italian, too.'

'Hey, fuck off. Seriously fuck off. I mean it.'

'. . .'

'. . .'

'Do you know the only band we could've been?'

'Who?'

'The Mary Chain.'

'The Mary Chain? How come?'

'Cause we're lazy shits and nobody likes us. They've made a fortune out of that.'

'Yeah, that's true. You especially. That would have been something, though, eh? Look, there's those two wee lassies away . . . Pity, I quite fancied the one with the Hamilton Accies top . . . *God, would you look at that, they're away with the Willie Miller Brothers, man.* How come the Willie Miller Brothers get all the women, eh? They're ugly bastards.'

'Don't ask me. You're the expert on women, Guiseppe.'

'Women . . . Ah, women . . . Many a good man's been ruined by a woman. Oh aye, they've fried more brains than the mushies, man. Many of life's great misconceptions revolve around women.'

'Tell me more, wee man.'

'I will. Right – the one about women being more mature than men. That's one for starters: pish. Another one – this strong, independent woman lark. That's bullshit. I met one of them once.'

'Did you?'

'I did. She was totally successful and that, earning loads of money, and you know what? Within two minutes of me meeting her for the first time she'd told me her entire life story. Steer well clear of them, man. They're just stupid wee lassies with wrinkles.'

'So I take it you got a knock-back.'

'Yeah, but that's beside the point. Said I was a contrary squirt with some kind of complex.'

'Ha ha. Nice to see she had a sense of humour.'

'That's the thing. Women don't have a good sense of humour. They just try to be witty.'

'My mam's got a good sense of humour.'

'But it's all that Jeremy Beadle stuff.'

'I love Jeremy Beadle, man.'

'Don't say that. Don't say that. You're selling yourself short.'

'How?'

'. . . You just are. I don't know. You just are.'

'You can be quite snobby and middle class at times, wee man.'

'What? Sorry? Did I hear you right there?'

'You heard me. You're snobby. All this kind of stuff. You don't like Jeremy Beadle cause everybody says you're not supposed to. Come on, the guy knows what's funny.'

'Fuck off. The guy is disturbing. I don't like him cause he's a total prick.'

'Sure, you've never even seen him in action.'

'I don't need to. He's detestable, man. As Oscar Wilde says, "If somebody looks a total prick, then it stands to reason they are a total prick". Don't talk about him. I feel ill.'

'. . .'

'. . .'

'Hey, look over there. Look, there's the guy that used to share the flat with Stan.'

'Oh no, so it is. The-man-with-the-cardboard-towel-under-his-bed.'

'Now there's a guy with an incredibly high sex drive.'

'Fuck off, he's just a chug-merchant . . . That towel was

disgusting, though, eh? He used to touch himself with that thing. Yeuch. Guy needs help, man.'

'I can't even look at him without that smell coming back.'

'You could smell it when you walked in the door, man.'

'Disgusting, it is.'

'Revolting.'

'. . .'

'. . .'

'Hey, wee man. You've agreed with me on something. When was the last time you did that?'

'No – I agree with you sometimes. On occasions.'

'Nah, never. What you do is when I say something you've either got to disagree with me or agree with me more than I do to the point where I'm supposed to think the opposite to what I've actually bloody well said . . . and don't you deny it.'

'Oh, it's all coming out now.'

'IT'S TRUE!'

'Will you keep your voice down? When you come away with things like that you can be quite embarrassing. I despair of you sometimes . . . but then you're Scottish – you're only partly to blame.'

'Well . . .'

'Well nothing. Shut up and get pissed and pretend you're a man.'

'. . .'

'. . .'

'Can't wait till the start of the season.'

'That's more like it. Look, are you coming through with us to see the boys this time or what?'

'Nah, no way. I support the local team.'

'Fuck off then. Mickey Mouse Hun Man.'

'That's me. Do you think that any of the antics we seen in the World Cup will have any affect on our beloved domestic game?'

'Nah, all that diving and fouling and arguing with referees'll never catch on here.'

'Ha ha. The wee man made a joke.'

'You just get fed up with all these Jimmy Hills telling us how crap the World Cup was.'

'It was great.'

'It was brilliant. Wish it was on every fucking week, man.'

'Pity the poor Trevors went out on penalties.'

'I know. How come they never got annihilated 52-0 like they deserved?'

'This time always brings out the hatred of the Trevors, eh?'

'Everybody hates the Trevors, man. It's a worldwide birthright. Mind the way Willie Ormond used to say "The English" like it was a disease or something. That was the best squad that.'

'Yeah. The thing is, though, if the Paddies can make the quarter finals and the Trevors can make the semis – then we should be able to win it.'

'Oh God, here we go, here we go. It's Ally MacLeod time. Look, the Scots, man – never. Never.'

'Nah, we should.'

'No way. The Scots are only good for soiling towels. That and inventing things. And nothing else needs to be invented. The Scots are a museum, man.'

'Gan you and dang, wee man.'

'It's the truth, man. Face it.'

'Pish. You're talking pish.'

'Chugland. That's what this place should be called. Chugland. Welcome to Chugland – the land of the chug. Do you know there are more men than women in this country? Every other country in the world has more women. Every other country apart from Chugland. Every other country in the world 2 – Chugland 1. It's like the scores, man. Gubbed . . . Hey, hey, hey – check what's come strolling in the door. That is one serious bit of heft.'

'Yeah, well serious.'

'Man, she's like Kathy Lloyd – perfect.'

'Hey, wait a minute, I know who that is, that's Eric's wee sister.'

'Fucking hell, so it is. When did she grow up?'

'Don't know. Haven't seen Eric for years. She must have been about fourteen the last time we seen her.'

'She certainly doesn't look fourteen now. Whoah!'

'Oh, wee man, look who she's with.'

'*God!* — not another of the Willie Miller Brothers.'

'There's nothing else for it, wee man. You're going to have to grow a moustache.'

'Fuck off. But she is something serious. I mind when we used to go round there she used to pat me on the bum all the time.'

'Yeah, I mind that. Strange wee lassie.'

'This isn't fair. Think about it: I look Italian; I've got an incredibly high sex drive; the most beautiful woman to walk into this place in five years used to pat me on the bum – and now she's hanging onto one of the Willie Miller Brothers! What else could go wrong? Tell me.'

'Well, if you insist, I'll tell you. I wasn't going to tell you, but I'll tell you.'

'What you on about?'

'Listen, Elsie up at the bar was telling us that that group of wee lassies over there think we're a couple of homos.'

'WHAT?'

'I'm telling you, wee man.'

'!!!'

'. . .'

'That is serious. That is well fucking serious. I can do without that. Right, tomorrow you are going out to get you a woman.'

'Eh – me?'

'Yeah, you. You work in a factory with three hundred of them. Pick one. Anything'll do.'

'Whatever happened to you and your incredibly high sex drive?'

'I'll get somebody. Don't you worry.'

'I'll tell you it's a crying shame that two men can't be seen to enjoy each other's company without folk thinking they're up each other's bums.'

'It's women that put these things about. Women. Men are never allowed to forget themselves, they've always to be on their guard. Hey, if women want equality they should come out and get rubbered and talk about football like they do in Brazil.'

'Difficult that, wee man. Women are social drinkers.'

'*Social drinkers?* Pah, the scum of the earth. "Oh no, I've had my two pints, that's my limit." God, I detest that shower. That's what it's like at my work when they go out for a drink. After a couple of bevs they're dandering their way down the road, man.'

'What? Unbelievable.'

'The purpose of drink is to get paralytic and talk pish.'

'True, wee man. And there's no finer exponent at either task than yourself. Here, want a fag?'

'God, when will you stop buying those cheapo fags? What are they this time? *Blue Windsor? Blue Windsor* in a red packet. That just about sums you up. How could I ever have been in a group with anyone who smoked *Blue Windsor* in a red packet? You know what your trouble is? You're un-rock-n-roll.'

'What?'

'You're un-rock-n-roll.'

'. . .'

'. . .'

'You mean I'm not degenerate.'

'Basically, yes.'

'Am I supposed to be ashamed of that or something?'

'Ha ha. I don't know. Think about it. Des from *Neighbours*. Look, think about it.'

'Jesus, but . . .'

'You're not Iggy Pop.'

'Neither's Iggy Pop.'

'I know but he used to be. You should buy yourself a leather jacket and grow your hair a bit.'

'You're absolutely rubbered the night, wee man.'

'Oh yeah. Right, who scored the Colombian goal against the Germans?'

'Eh, Rincon.'

'Just testing.'

'Right, wee man. I'll tell you one Scottish characteristic you've got in overabundance.'

'What's that?'

'You never shut up . . . There you go.'

'God, you know nothing. *You know nothing.* You ever seen Italians, man? Now that is what you call talking. All that mamma mia shit. I love it. That is my all-time number one ultimate fantasy: an Italian woman screaming at me for five minutes and threatening to cut my balls off. Passion, man, passion. I love it. Them or the French.'

'I like wee French lassies myself. They can wear jumpers and look cool.'

'That's this country, man. *Marks and Spencers* jumpers that are too wee for you. See if you shouted out "Who's wearing a Marks and Spencers jumper that's too wee for them?" half this country would stick its hand up.'

'That's a fact, wee man.'

'AND WILL YOU STOP CALLING ME THAT! You're precisely half an inch taller than me.'

'. . .'

'. . .'

'I look a lot taller than you. Everybody says that. You look wee. Everybody says that.'

'Nah, you know the only reason you look taller than me? The only reason you look taller than me is cause you don't have shoulders. See, I've got the right build for my height. I've got shoulders, you haven't. I'm lean and slim, you're just skinny.'

'Eh . . .'

'The eighties was the decade of the shoulders and you never had any. That just about sums up your contribution. You'd have been all right in the sixties, nobody had shoulders back then.'

'Have I any hope for the nineties?'

'Nah, shouldn't think so. Let's face it. You're a lost cause. I think it'll be . . . arses. Yeah, arses. I find myself noticing them more and more.'

'Big ones or wee ones?'

'Eh . . . wee for men. Tight and tiny, like mine. Big for women. Massive. Big as you can get. And another thing . . .! Hey, wait a minute.'

'. . .'
'!!!'
'. . .'
'!!!'
'. . .'
'What's he playing this for?'
'Eh, I requested it earlier. I thought it might help you wind down after our World Cup post-mortem.'
'FUCKING GODLIKE!!! FUCKING GODLIKE!!! I haven't heard this for years, man. Oh, brilliant.'
'Eh . . . you can sit down, wee man. There's no need to get just quite so excited.'
'This guy . . . a genius, man. There's no other word for it.'
'One of the best records ever made.'
'Hey, listening to it just now, I can't think of anything that's better. Can you? Can you tell me anything that's better? Are you trying to tell me there's anything better? You can't, can you? You can't. Two and a half minutes of total perfection . . . Look, everybody here's into it. Look at them. See them. They're into it.'
'I know. I'm watching them.'
'They're tapping their fingers, tapping their toes. They're into it. Look at them. Oh, they're beautiful. They're actually looking better. Look at them. Savour it, just savour it.'
'. . .'
'. . .'
'That was good. Eh, wee man.'
'I am drained. Awesome is the only word I feel like using. Awesome.'
'Outstanding.'
'Nah, awesome. Awesome's the word.'
'Right, are we going or what?'
'Awesome. Yeah, I suppose so. Hey, don't hassle me. I'm ready.'
'Come on then. Away to your bed.'
'Away to think about that lassie with the Hamilton Accies top and Eric's wee sister.'
'Wee man, pack it in.'

'That's what my dad used to say to us. Used to bang on the fucking door and shout "PACK IT IN, SON, AND GO TO SLEEP! NOW!" Frightened the fucking life out of me when he did that.'

'Hey, come on. Don't start.'

'It's this fucking country, man. It does it to you. "A million Scots every day/Put on a sock and chug away/Scots love to chug." It's all they're fucking good for.'

'Eh, sorry, missus. Wee bit bevvied you know. Come on, you. Let's get out of here and try not to fall into any hedges the night.'

'Hey, remember we better get our act ready and go this time.'

'What?'

'What do you mean "what"? The next World Cup. What do you think I'm talking about?'

'Sure. Yeah. I'm going.'

'. . .'

'. . .'

'Do you know? I've been thinking.'

'God, not again.'

'Nah, do you realise – this is interesting this – do you realise that we drink more than everybody these days?'

'Eh . . .'

'Think about it: everybody's married and settled down; everybody's moved away; the dopeheads never go out; even the alcoholics stopped.'

'They had to.'

'Yeah, but think about it . . . We drink more than everybody.'

'. . .'

'. . .'

'Amazing.'

'Told you.'

'Boring bastards, they are, eh?'

'Yeah, boring bastards. Well boring bastards.'

'. . .'

'. . .'